Immersive
LOVE

Angelic Williams

Halo
PUBLISHING
INTERNATIONAL

Halo Publishing International
8000 W Interstate 10, #600
San Antonio, Texas 78230

First Edition, September 2022
Printed in the United States of America
ISBN: 978-1-63765-267-1
Library of Congress Control Number: 2022912560

The information contained within this book is strictly for informational purposes. Unless otherwise indicated, all the names, characters, businesses, places, events and incidents in this book are either the product of the author's imagination or used in a fictitious manner. Any resemblance to actual persons, living or dead, or actual events is purely coincidental.

Halo Publishing International is a self-publishing company that publishes adult fiction and non-fiction, children's literature, self-help, spiritual, and faith-based books. We continually strive to help authors reach their publishing goals and provide many different services that help them do so. We do not publish books that are deemed to be politically, religiously, or socially disrespectful, or books that are sexually provocative, including erotica. Halo reserves the right to refuse publication of any manuscript if it is deemed not to be in line with our principles. Do you have a book idea you would like us to consider publishing? Please visit www.halopublishing.com for more information.

To my mother, Ella, who loved and accepted all of me, even the parts I've yet to love, unconditionally.

May 13, 1948 — April 7, 2022

Contents

Chapter 1   11
I Found Your Beanie

Chapter 2   19
Did You Get My Gift?

Chapter 3   33
I Bought One of Each

Chapter 4   44
All-Nighters

Chapter 5   52
Pinky Caressing

Chapter 6   60
Subway Stations

Chapter 7   72
Diesel

Chapter 8   84
Farmers Markets

Chapter 9   100
Massages

Chapter 10   112
I Hated That Dress

Chapter 11   120
King of Anything

Chapter 12   126
Magic Hands

Chapter 13   134
You Never Liked Parasailing

Chapter 14   142
Ladies Pavilion Sunsets

Chapter 15   151
Pineapple of Hospitality

Chapter 16   159
Ferrari Bombs

Chapter 17   170
Frozen on a Balcony

Chapter 18   181
Radio City

Chapter 19   191
Stolen Kisses at the Flagpole

Chapter 20   197
300-Percent Tip

Chapter 21   205
Twenty-Three Minutes Late

Chapter 22   216
Shake Shack

Chapter 23   230
Footloose

Acknowledgments   241

Chapter 1

I Found Your Beanie

Mmm, what time is it?

Viv's hungover, her hand fumbling around the top of the nightstand, when suddenly she is interrupted by the familiar yet foreign touch of another body next to her. Instinctually, her fingers locate the phone.

It's 8:26 a.m. Time to go.

Truth be told, it didn't matter what time it was. It was time to go. Last night, she'd had another fulfilling conquest. As she slowly collected her things, Viv recalled the events of the prior evening, and as with all the others, she felt it fade to black.

***

Viv was enjoying an old-fashioned made with Eagle Rare Kentucky Straight Bourbon Whiskey at one of her favorite establishments, That Other Place. TOP, as it was affectionately known, was a quaint spot tucked just off the main road in town. Heavy wooden doors carved from reclaimed wood were the only way you'd find it. The owner, Sylvie, was staunchly against having signage on the outside. You found out by word of mouth.

Inside, there were a handful of cozy booths made of navy-blue velvet and gold tables to go along with the bar seating. There was always a musk of cigar and cigarette smoke in the air that clung to the clothes of patrons. The decor transported you back a century to *The Great Gatsby* era. The uniform for the staff consisted of a crisp white shirt with a black vest and suspenders for the men, and black and gold flapper dresses for the women. With an impressively expansive mahogany bar and a dress code for its guests, it was the perfect place to unplug from the city.

TOP was a venue that suited Viv's needs. Discreet. Beautifully designed. Equally beautiful clientele. She sat facing the door in her usual booth by the only window. Best vantage point. Viv had a particular type—mysterious. A story to tell. Beautiful eyes. Long hair. A mind for creativity. Ernie, the bartender, knew all the clientele. If a guest entered who was both available and queer, he'd tilt his head to the left. If Viv was interested, she'd tilt her glass back in his direction. That was the cue to put their drink on her tab.

Inevitably, the guest would end up in her booth. Viv was a charmer. She had an energy that lit up any room and disguised her guarded heart. She had piercing hazel eyes that made any woman feel as if she were the most important thing in the world. She hated to talk about herself, though she rarely had to. Most people knew who she was. Vivienne Roche, the wildly successful, homegrown immersive artist. Initially known for her expressive impressionistic paintings, à la Leonid Afremov, she was often prompted to talk about how she shifted into adding elements of performance and technology into her work. Never wanting to appear pompous, she indulged her company with what, at this point, had become rehearsed answers. Honest, but rehearsed. What wasn't rehearsed was how genuinely intrigued Viv was to learn about her newest companion.

Belle, thirty-two, was originally from Amsterdam. At five foot six with burnt-auburn hair and light-blue eyes, she was easily the standout of the night. Rarely did she have time to socialize or have a drink due to the nature of her job. She was a junior vice president at an investment banking firm, a traditionally taxing job, both in mental energy and hours. She was on the fast track to becoming the youngest senior vice president in the company's history. Though the subject matter bored Viv, she listened intently, captivated by Belle's passion. Surprisingly, Belle shifted gears and shared that despite being known as a shark in her field, in her youth, she had shown a much softer side as an accomplished singer and pianist.

It was just the opening Viv was looking for. "That's such a shame," she said, shaking her head.

Belle looked at her puzzled.

Viv stared intently into her eyes while gently intertwining their hands. "Wasting such beautiful fingers crunching numbers when you could be making music."

***

Viv glanced back at the rays of sun streaking in through the shades and falling onto the floor, grazing over Belle's nipples as she stirred quietly. Viv sighed. It was always this part that softened her cold heart.

Why can't I just stay? Make conversation? Order breakfast like a normal person? Maybe just this one time I can... No!

With her wits about her, Viv was ready to leave. She made just enough noise to wake Belle, who spoke in the tone of someone who'd spent most of the night trying to catch their breath.

Barely present, her voice tiredly quavering as she spoke, Belle inquired, "Leaving already?"

"Yeeaaah." Viv slyly stood up to button her pants. "Big show's coming up. I like to get in early to check the progress."

Increasingly alert, Belle turned onto her stomach. "Hmph, okay. I don't want to be a distraction." She smiled, playfully tempting Viv to stay.

"You're the best type of distraction," Viv said as she leaned her knee back onto the bed and planted a kiss on Belle's lips, "but I do have to go. I'll text you later."

The crisp morning air greeted Viv as she inhaled sharply through her nose. With a grin on her face, she left feeling energized. It was the chase that she enjoyed. She replayed the night in her head again and again as she crossed the Golden Gate Bridge back into San Francisco. Carefully tracing her word choices, making sure she'd stayed on script. Nothing in the margins. Business in, business out. The revolving and ever-expanding Rolodex of female companions was enough for her. Whether it be travel sex on a business trip or a night like last night, there wasn't much more she could desire.

The drive back across the bridge always brought things back into focus. Peering to the left at the San Francisco skyline poking through the infamous fog, she took a deep breath and exhaled her anxiety about any potential missteps.

I own this city, and this city owns me.

A sly grin crept across her face. The view never got old. Inevitably, the nostalgia of simpler times flowed through her mind. She turned on a '90s radio playlist on Spotify and sang her heart out to SWV's "I'm So Into You." This was her comfort zone. One with the music, she saw beauty and light in the world in a way that opened her mind to possibilities. Or the darkness it held. It depended on the song. Viv had learned the power of music at an early age. Its ability to be a common thread between strangers or to tell a story in ways that few could articulate. It was the great equalizer across cultures. An equalizer to which she found herself magically drawn.

She playfully serenaded other drivers on the road as she passed by. Some laughed. Others stared in bewilderment. But what did it matter? Adulthood felt as if it were just shuttling from one responsibility to another. Why not have fun on the way?

Back in the city, she illegally double-parked to hop into her local Jamba Juice and pick up her order.

"Hey Mario!" she saluted him as she breezed her way across the floor.

"Goooooood morning, chief! Successful landing?" Mario, who typically worked the early morning shifts, was used to Viv's post-sex breakfast visits.

"Always! Couldn't show my face if it wasn't," she joked.

"Sixteen Strawberries Wild and a Belgian waffle freshly warmed for you," he said, handing it across the counter. "Man, if I could live one day like you…"

"You couldn't handle it." She smiled through her words as she turned to walk towards the door.

He really couldn't handle it, she thought, sipping on her smoothie as she finished the uneventful four-block drive home.

Once inside the elevator, with the PH button pressed, she slumped against the walls. For Viv, the only time she felt alive was in the company of another woman or with her art.

The moments in between all felt painfully gray. It's a wonder to many how that could be, with the life she lived. As the doors opened to the penthouse, she slowly came back to life. Still sipping on her smoothie, she twirled and ran her hands along the floor-to-ceiling glass in her living room.

She loved this building. Designed by one of her favorite architects, Jeanne Gang, the Mira Building was pure art. Each floor plan was the same, but twisted twenty degrees clockwise from the floor plan below it; the end result was more a sculpture than just another phallic symbol in the sky. From the moment the design was announced, she knew she had to live there. The instant presales were available, she'd raced to call the leasing agent and put a deposit down for one of the penthouses.

She ran her fingers across her cherry-stained credenza, stopping at the end to pick up an eight-and-a-half-by-eleven framed photo of her parents on their wedding day. "Good morning, Mom and Dad," she said, kissing both of their faces before turning to take in her not-so-humble abode. It was a far cry from the way she was raised.

The only child of Geraldine and Henri Roche, Viv was a blend of art and science. Geraldine was an accomplished oil painter and sculptor in her own right. Though she regularly had gallery showings, she rarely intended to expand her profile beyond the Bay Area, unlike her precocious daughter.

Young Viv was regularly spotted peering between the adults huddled around Geraldine's five-foot-seven frame, completely enchanted by the way she swayed in one of her signature floral dresses. Geraldine's sparkling eyes would shine through her oversized round glasses as she described the inspiration behind her work. When Viv wasn't ear hustling, she'd sneak glasses of wine from the catering tray by the kitchen, with the other artists' kids, to try and understand why all the adults couldn't stand not having a glass in their hands at all times. Countless openings. Countless sips. Same reaction.

Bleeeeck! Still gross! I don't get it. I'll never like this stuff like they do...

Henri could always be spotted about an arm's length away from his wife. He'd step in and schmooze with guests when she would give him the "I need a break" look. His job, unlike Geraldine's, never brought such fanfare and face-to-face adoration from the masses. Rather, he did the thankless work that enriches everyday modern-human life. He was a semiconductor engineer at Intel.

When they weren't at Geraldine's gallery openings, Viv would watch intently as Henri explained the experiments he was working on, using extra scraps brought home from the office. He would buy old remotes, TVs, typewriters, telephones—you name it. He'd show Viv what each piece did and challenge her to put them back together in working condition. Viv often attributed her anal retentiveness to these challenges. When Henri first introduced the challenge with a remote, she would lazily skip over pieces she didn't deem important, only to be frustrated later when she couldn't complete the task. But with each success, she "graduated" to the next level, her attention to detail increasing with each step.

Through Viv's eyes, it was a charmed life in their cramped two-bedroom apartment in the Mission District. She often thought of her parents as penguins, in that they mated for life. They became high school sweethearts after Geraldine's friends dared her to ask Henri to the Sadie Hawkins Day dance during their senior year. Geraldine was in the popular group and participated in the music and arts programs, while scrawny Henri was a quiet mathlete. Though she originally asked him out because she hated backing down from a dare, he charmed her with his personality and smooth dance moves. They were inseparable. For a growing Viv, it was a rose-colored view of what love should be. A bubble, in fact, as she'd later find out. Her parents were the exception, not the rule.

Ting…ting! The sound of a text broke Viv's trance. It was Gabby, Viv's agent and publicist.

Gabby: Walkthrough and interview at the gallery at four sharp. Be nice.

Gabby: And don't forget to eat your waffle. I can't deal with low blood sugar V today.

Viv: How do you know I didn't stay home last night?

Gabby: Tell that to someone who hasn't booked interviews for the past twelve years. I know exactly how you shake off your pre-interview jitters.

Viv: Yeah, yeah, yeah.

Gabby: Tell me I'm lying.

Viv: Goodbye, Gab. I'll see you at four.

Viv opened the top drawer of the credenza and pulled out a new pack of Marlboro Golds and her orange lighter. The crisp smell of the freshly lit cigarette filled the space. Viv held it at her side as she wandered to her closet, dragging her feet as if she were a kid punished to a time-out. She took a second to scan the entire room before taking a lingering drag of her cigarette and letting out a long, slow exhale.

I hate this part.

Chapter 2

Did You Get My Gift?

Gabby tapped her pen on her clipboard. *At four. At four.*

It was 3:57 p.m. and still no Viv.

"I don't know why you do this to yourself. You know she's probably pulling into the garage right now and smoking in the car, waiting until *exactly* four. Besides, it's Susie. She always shows up for Susie," Lorenzo said to Gabby.

Lorenzo was Viv's handler and driver. He accompanied her to every event, interview, and public-speaking engagement. His primary job was to get Viv to and from her appearances; his secondary, to keep Viv's mental state calm. Zo knew Viv's issues intimately. More than with any of her other shortcomings, Viv went to great lengths to hide not only her general tension, but also her anxiety when dealing with the formalities and expectations of being a world-renowned artist and local phenomenon.

Gabby hired Zo after Viv ceased being the consummate, albeit reluctant, professional two years before. After she'd no-showed several engagements, half-assed commission work, and lost the signature passion that captivated audiences. Rumors began to spread that Viv had lost her Midas touch. She'd hated the idea of a handler when Gabby suggested it as a solution. Viv must've rejected over thirty applicants before settling on Lorenzo.

***

"I don't need a babysitter," she snapped at Gabby when they first discussed it.

"Yes, you do. I wouldn't suggest it if I thought 'badass Viv that drives me crazy but always shows up' was going to magically reappear tomorrow. But she's not. We both know this." Gabby paused and then softened her tone as she continued, "We all need a little help here and there."

Viv's eyes lowered to focus on the concrete floor she was sitting on, her back resting against the wall with her arms crossed over her knees. "Not me. Not like this."

Gabby crouched down to meet her eye to eye. "I know you don't," she said as she grabbed Viv's hands, staring at her sternly, "but we're still fucking doing it."

"Fine"—Viv sighed—"but *I* get to pick her."

"HIM. Or them," Gabby replied sharply.

Viv looked at her, initially confused, and then rolled her eyes.

"I'm not gonna let you fuck this up. Literally."

Zo was different from all the other candidates. On the outside, he fit the bill—six foot four, slicked-back curly hair, black slacks, and matching blazer with a navy-blue shirt. He was Colombian, in his midforties, and first-generation American. He looked cold and intimidating, but once he sat down, he treated the interview as if it were a conversation with an old friend, rather than listing off the rules he planned to enforce. The other candidates had all dealt with high-profile personalities who had drug addictions, were flippant spenders, had gambling problems, had flaming tempers, or were Hollywood divas. Viv was none of those things. Sure, she had her quirks but none warranted the types of controls other applicants were suggesting; namely, weekly allowances, curfews, and safe words.

Zo had done his homework. On the day of an event, Viv needed to be picked up and dropped off. She needed to get to her studio five hours early to run through everything from all angles. She'd want to make sure that the paint was mixed properly. That the gesso had been dried to her satisfaction. That the brushes were fresh. She was the type of control freak for whom her crew could work without going crazy. She had a rhythm, a cadence that was always predictable. Though they never understood it, it was easy to meet her expectations.

After a show, if Viv left with a companion, Zo was to drive her to the Intercontinental Hotel on Howard Street, where he'd already arranged a reservation. Her usual corner suite was normally booked months in advance. The reservation was always for two nights since she never checked out on time and hotels gave her the freedom to indulge in morning sex and to leave at the late-checkout time she requested.

Gabby continuously tried to get Viv to agree to hiring a stylist, but she always adamantly refused. She only allowed one person to dress and style her for events and had no interest in working with someone else. She only bent her rule if it was a photo shoot for a magazine.

Before a show she needed her go-go juice (pineapple and tequila) exactly thirty minutes before showtime. Enough time for her buzz to set in. On interview days, which Gabby booked incessantly leading up to a new show, Viv would only show up at the time dictated and not a second sooner.

Zo respected all of these quirks. His goal was never to control Viv. His goal was to keep her inside the margins. Business in, business out.

***

Like clockwork, Viv entered triumphantly through the rear of the gallery, flashing her megawatt smile.

"You're killin' me, Smalls," Gabby said, rolling her neck, relieved yet flustered.

"You love me," Viv said, planting a kiss on her cheek as she zoomed by. "Where is she? Main space?"

"Yup!" Gabby yelled.

It's go time.

"Susie Q! Long time no see," Viv greeted her guest with out-stretched arms for a hug.

"The famous Ms. Roche." Susie gripped her tight and gave her a kiss on both cheeks.

"Famous or infamous?" Viv quipped.

"Depends on who you ask," Susie replied smiling.

They both knew, in circles where Viv was less popular, her name was bastardized to be pronounced *roach* instead of *r-oh-sh*.

They settled themselves in the middle of the elevated seating for her audience. Viv's anxiety ticked down a couple of notches as it was much easier to talk to Susie than any other interviewer.

Susana Gonzalez was one of the premier art critics in San Francisco. She had covered Viv's shows for over a decade, gaining firsthand knowledge on Viv's meteoric rise. Susie conducted Viv's first big interview after a video of her went viral. For a while, she was the only person with whom Viv agreed to interview, making her featured stories that much more coveted by publishers.

***

Viv was classically trained in portraiture and landscapes, outside of her formal education, which she referred to as "boring school." She'd followed in her mother's footsteps and attended Parsons School of Design in New York City, majoring in fine art. The fast-paced nature of the city matched her zest for life. She began infusing some of that energy into her art as her style veered more into the abstract. Whereas Geraldine's paintings would capture you with the dimension of her oil paintings, Viv's stood out because everything looked as if it were in motion. Her style was part impressionist, part surrealist. What would the Empire State Building look like in a hurricane if it had the structural integrity of a palm tree? Viv painted it. Trees with leaves made of lava? Viv painted it. Each idea wackier than the last, but it was so flawlessly executed that you believed it could be real.

Despite growing a decent-sized following after graduating in 2007, she returned to San Francisco to build her career there. She split her time between helping Geraldine with her openings, as she did when she was a kid, and working on her own inspirations. Viv wanted to build an artist persona that was different from the one she developed in New York.

One thing that did follow Viv from New York? The party. Aside from her work, which dominated most of her time, she was known for throwing elaborate and hedonistic paint parties. Once she was settled in her new studio space in SOMA, she continued the tradition.

The setup was pretty straightforward. She'd cover her entire studio, walls included, with canvas tarps. She'd set up individual easels for people who actually wanted to paint and scattered paint stations around the room for people who wanted to paint on the tarps or each other. Combine those elements with a ton of liquor and banging music, and you've got yourself a party like no other. Viv greeted everyone who came through the door, whether she knew them or not, with the same big grin and a hug. She'd saunter around her paint playground in a skimpy bathing suit, allowing her guests to paint on her as they pleased.

Once the clock struck midnight, she'd up the ante, bringing out glow-in-the-dark body paint. This was Viv's favorite part as she was normally the first one to the bins. One night, she was noticeably absent from the fray. Byron, one of Viv's childhood friends, took note and went to find her. He checked the usual spots when looking for her—out front for a smoke, at the bar for a refill, and in the alley for a quickie with the flavor of the night. No dice. He scanned through the crowd of about a hundred guests for his hostess with the mostest.

He found himself at the rear of the studio, confused as to where she could be. As one song transitioned to another, he swore he could hear her singing, but from where? He ran his hands along the tarp-covered walls until he felt a door handle. He slipped underneath the tarp and peered through the small window. Inside was Viv. Unhinged. Free.

He'd seen Viv paint a million times before, but not like this. As in every inch of her studio, this tiny room was also equipped with surround sound. He watched in amazement as the lyrics from "Empire State of Mind" by JAY-Z and Alicia Keys pumped through the speakers. Viv stood in the center of a semicircle of three easels and was painting as she sang along. Her back was to Byron.

He watched in awe as her fingers flicked paint to the beat. The brushes landed randomly on the canvas, based on the way she moved to the music. She moved precisely and delicately to the softer parts of the track, slowly amping up with the beat, splattering paint across the canvases. Immersed in a song that was a love letter to her second home, her motions slowly faded with the music. What was left were three completely different canvases that captured Viv's spirit and all the emotions she felt during that song. He backed away as she set up three new canvases as the next song started.

Twenty minutes later, Viv returned to the party with renewed energy, unaware that Byron had seen her secret art. Or that he, an early adopter of tech, had filmed it on his newly debuted $600 iPhone. In his spare time, Byron was an early blogger on YouTube. His primary videos consisted of San Francisco nightlife or celebrity rants.

Viv knew that Byron reviewed her paint parties, but she didn't pay much attention to it until she eventually began receiving dozens of texts about her "Empire State of Mind" paintings, along with emails requesting her to paint new songs and asking how one or all three pieces could be purchased. Confused, she pulled up Byron's YouTube page and watched his review of her party. Her jaw dropped once she saw the footage of her hidden room. It dropped even farther, and a lump in her throat formed when she saw that the video already had *two million* views. The next day, that number jumped to fifteen million. Media requests soon followed.

Viv, as she normally would, turned to her mom for advice. She understood how to create and curate art, but knew nothing about how to handle the media attention she was receiving. Geraldine suggested they go on a walk through Golden Gate Park to help her daughter clear her head. Viv's worries and fears flooded out of her as they walked. With each word that escaped her lips, her breath became more labored. Her voice went higher. Her anxiety was wrapping itself around her throat the way a snake kills its prey.

Geraldine put her arm around Viv, pulling her close and rubbing her arm. "Just breathe, baby. It's all going to be fine. I promise. Just take some deep breaths."

Once Viv calmed herself, Geraldine gave her two pieces of advice: one, to tell her story before someone told it for her, and two, to interview with the up-and-coming reporter Susana Gonzalez, who was mentored by one of Geraldine's journalist colleagues. She wanted Viv to be her own artist, but also wanted to make sure she had a watchful eye and trusted outlet for her daughter's debut feature story.

The same was true when it came time to pick an agent. Geraldine only took referrals from trusted contemporaries and friends. With Viv, she interviewed each agent to find the right fit. Gabrielle Kachabi was the perfect choice. She was in her early thirties, of Iranian and British descent, and had the drive and tenacity that Geraldine was looking for to manage the dynamic triad of Viv's personality, anxiety, and career trajectory. She wasn't driven by rubbing elbows with the latest viral sensation. She was focused on business and making sure Viv's career stayed on the straight and narrow as prescribed by Geraldine: "No drugs.

No commissioned pieces for modern-day fascists. No letting someone other than Viv control her narrative as an artist. Business in, business out." Viv, who was notoriously uninterested in the business part of the art world, needed a ying to her yang. That was Gabby.

What Viv didn't know was just how good Gabby would be at her job. Suddenly her face was everywhere. She had a schedule that Gabby had booked weeks in advance. Daytime talk shows, late-night talk shows, and halftime shows at stadiums. Four, sometimes five, flights in a week. Viv received special requests globally for everything from appearances at cultural events to audiences with world leaders. Everyone wanted to see the viral sensation in person to see if she lived up to the hype. Viv was up to the task and consistently delivered.

She became known as the most accessible artist. Because her art was produced on the spot, she could do more shows than the average creator. What started as painting to songs on demand quickly shifted toward putting her unique point of view out into the world and providing personal, political, or simple social commentary. She always put her signature Viv touch on it, drawing people further into her mystique.

Despite her growing fame, she remained the same Viv that she'd always been. Though Gabby always billed her shows formally as a Vivienne Roche production, Viv was adamant that informally she'd always go by Viv. She was frequently seen taking BART or a MUNI bus around the city, much to Gabby's disapproval. It cheapened the brand that she was working to build for Viv. When Viv protested, Gabby suggested a bodyguard accompany her if she *had* to be on public transit.

"What's the point in that?" Viv questioned before quickly giving up. "Fine. We'll do it your way. I'll drive my car from now on."

Gabby raised her eyebrows. "That beat-up hunk o'junk? Nope. No way. You need to get a new one. I'll help you shop for one."

Viv threw her hands up in surrender.

"Perfect. Let's go over the schedule. I've made some changes."

Despite the new rules and restrictions, all Viv had to worry about was creating art. The rest happened in the background. It was white noise to her. The schedule matched Viv's frenetic energy, but it still wasn't enough.

A true artist never stops evolving. That's how she was raised. She needed to push the envelope. Push herself. She wanted to put on her own shows, not just gallery openings. She trained intensely with aerial and trapeze artists, to take flight during her shows and provide a full experience for the audiences, instead of just standing still with her backs to them while she painted. They set up different platforms for her to swing between. She was inspired by watching the former Warriors' mascot, Thunder, bounce off trampolines as a kid, and Viv incorporated that into her shows as well. What was once three canvases surrounding a painter evolved into an arena of canvases, trampolines, and landings. In the middle of it all was Viv.

To accommodate her new direction, she bought the neighboring warehouse, which was adjacent to her studio space, with the help of her parents and the Great Recession that sent real estate values tumbling. She connected her former studio to her new space in order to create a space that was unique to her. Totaling 10,000 square feet now, she converted her original studio into her gallery, which was open to the public.

On the opposite end, the space was split into two areas. The rear was a much more chaotic scene as it housed the various canvases, frames, paint, and a small workshop to build custom items for the arena. The front was all business; it was for Gabby and her assistants and contained desks, couches for meetings, a rack of outfits for Viv, and most noticeably, a large schedule on the wall for Viv's various social engagements, interviews, and shows. The walls quickly became adorned with large prints of magazine covers featuring Viv, quotes from interviews, and photos of Viv with people she considered "real celebrities."

In the center, she built the arena she envisioned. At its essence, it was fairly straightforward. Two rows of leather chairs reserved for VIPs sat in front of glorified black bleachers for the general public. In front of the seats was the skeleton of the arena. It had the beige floor that doubled as a trampoline on which Viv could bounce, Viv's harness hanging from a skinny silver-metal track, and a black-metal frame system with quarter-sized notches that ran along the full length of the arena and hung from the ceiling. The interlocking notches in the frame allowed for as much customization as she wanted. She wanted to build what she called an Erector Set arena, which was a throwback to her nights building different structures with Henri after dinner.

Depending on the type of show, they'd arrange the tracks at different locations, at times closer together, at others farther apart. The canvas size would vary from eighteen by twenty-four to eight by eight. Viv would sketch out her vision and give it to the foreman of her studio crew to bring to fruition. They'd work through the best places for Viv to land and change paints and brushes.

With so much customization, each show was different from the last. Going to one of Viv's shows wasn't just about the art itself. It was about what you felt watching Viv create it. Her crew worked tirelessly with her over the years, developing a silent language; based on the motions she made with her feet, they knew how to control her movements behind the scenes, when to lift her more, when to give more slack, or when to swing her in a certain direction.

With each flip, each brushstroke, each flick of paint, Viv was unrestrained, expressing every ounce of emotion held within the songs blaring throughout the gallery and into her earpiece. She used every part of her body as the brush. Her hair, her feet. It was ethereal; breathtaking, most would say. For the one-of-a-kind pieces produced during the performance, after each show a silent auction was held while Viv sipped champagne with her guests in the gallery at the after-party. Viv easily walked away from each show with six figures to show for her tireless hours spent in the studio.

It was never really about the money for her. When she was performing, she felt free. Free from judgment. Free from responsibilities. Free from her worries.

At first glance, it may appear that Viv prioritized art over anything else. That may be true, but she didn't prioritize it over any*one* else. Every Wednesday night was game night at her parents' place, and every Sunday they had dinner together. No matter what. Viv's parents were still the center of her world, and she theirs. It was the stability she needed when everything around her was changing so quickly. Geraldine would help her think through her point of view for each show, while Henri would help her think through the tactical elements to set up the arena and maximize the experience. In the beginning, she needed more coaching.

"But what if they don't think I'm as good as you, Mom?" she asked one day before a show.

Geraldine grabbed her daughter's face delicately with both hands. "Your job isn't to give them *Geraldine's daughter*. Your job is to give them VIV. Only you can do that."

It wasn't long before she tapped Henri for more of his expertise. Viv hated wasting paint, even on the trampoline floor; she wanted to find a way to use the trampoline as both a canvas and a launchpad. No wasted space. Henri tapped some of his engineering friends for help while Viv asked some of her friends from school who worked in textiles. They'd worked for over a year, aside from her shows and engagements, trying to find the correct balance between buoyancy and structural integrity. Henri spent many evenings laughing at his daughter flying from canvas to canvas. They eventually perfected it, but it never debuted.

Until now.

***

"So tell me about this show," Susana asked, sitting in one of the audience's seats.

"It's going to be like NOTHING you've seen me do before," Viv said confidently.

"That's a pretty bold statement coming from you," Susana replied while taking notes.

Viv shrugged. "You know I like to push the envelope each time."

"If I'm not mistaken, this is the first *original* point-of-view piece you've done in almost two years…since October 2017, correct?" Susana asked, albeit rhetorically. Both were well aware that Viv had favored themed shows in the past, whether it be Valentine's Day or Beyoncé's new album.

"Yes, it's called *Immersive Love*. It discusses the variety of forms that love can take—joy, excitement, wonder, heartbreak, reconciliation, and the unbreakable bond formed between two people." Viv spoke with her hands, as she tended to, almost painting a picture in the air. "The name was also important. *Immersed* versus *submersed*. Something that is submerged is built to withstand that pressure, like a submarine. But when you immerse something, it's by an external force. That's what this show's about. A love that is struggling to survive against all of the outside forces trying to keep it below the surface."

"And where are you drawing inspiration from? Your parents?"

"Excuse me?" Viv's eyes darted to the ceiling and then back at Susana. *This wasn't in the prep questions.*

"I mean, Viv, let's be honest; your reputation precedes you. You've never *really* been in love, have you?" Susana's eyes lowered. She was pressing.

Viv's blood began to boil. Her mind started racing. She leaned toward Susana's recorder. "I love my art. And sex." Viv stopped the recording. "We're done here."

Viv rose and stomped quickly down the stands and across the studio, towards the garage to retrieve her car. Steam was practically coming out of her ears. The eyes of everyone in the studio were glued to Viv.

Gabby's hands extended as Viv neared. "What happened?" she asked. Susana was the only interviewer whom Viv actually liked.

"She poked the fucking bear," Viv scoffed as she walked by. "This shit better be out-fucking-standing for the show next week!" she yelled while leaving the studio.

Chapter 3

I Bought One of Each

The week leading up to the show, Viv did the unthinkable. She stayed home.

She wasn't at any of the typical social venues she frequented on different nights of the week. She wasn't in the studio nitpicking over every detail with the stage crew. She didn't even bother to call or text Gabby once the teaser interview was published. Viv usually scoured over every word choice, the photos used in the feature, and every other detail imaginable. Not this time. She never actually read it.

***

The night following the interview, Viv barely slept. Sitting in dim lighting in her living room, she stared out at her view overlooking the bay. For a moment, she became engrossed in the Bay Lights. What was once intended to be a temporary art piece, the installation spanned the western portion of the Bay Bridge, programmed LED lights affixed to the bridge's tension cables. An algorithm controls the light show so that it plays on a loop. But at a passing glance, which is what most people gave it, the lights looked as if they were dancing across the bridge and having the time of their lives.

Viv sighed, grabbed the Macallan Scotch whisky, which she'd poured herself some time ago and set on the minibar in the corner, and pressed her head against the cool glass.

What the fuck am I doing? People seem to love this themed shit. It's still me. Even if it is watered down. They still show up.

Leaving the window, she slumped onto one of her two wrap-around, gray-denim couches. She stared up at two huge eight-by-eight canvases from a previous show. Black canvases with deep blue, orange, and gold streaks and bits of paint captured every bit of emotion that Viv had the night she'd painted them. Each with its own unique emotional signature. As at other shows, they were bid on and won, but the winning bidder donated them back to Viv, believing that she deserved to keep them for her private collection. She swirled her remaining Scotch, listening to the ice clink against the glass in between sips. It started getting quiet in Viv's head as she reminisced about that night.

Fuck...I need to stay busy.

The ensuing days were spread across every square inch of that two-thousand-square-foot penthouse. She did countless reps on her over-the-door pull-up bar, spent endless hours on her Peloton bike, and worked night after night in her mini-arena setup in one of the bedrooms. This was made possible by the extremely high ceilings in the penthouse units. Equipped with a hydraulic harness apparatus and a six-by-six trampoline, she'd loft herself in the air, bouncing from wall to wall with fresh-out-the-box brushes in her hand. While unable to reach the same heights as those in the arena, the floating feeling was what she was seeking. Letting her energy flow through her veins into the bristles of the brush, she felt snippets of peace in her mind. When she was off like this, nothing she created ever felt like her. She'd paint over her work with gesso and shift to her workouts while she waited for it to dry.

Similar to the drag queens she loved and frequently patronized, the arena was the armor between her and the world, the place she portrayed her art persona and masked her everyday self. You can be whoever you want to be at that moment; the rest of the world doesn't matter as long as you're on that stage.

Day after day, workout after workout, drink after drink, Susana's words haunted her, replaying over and over in her mind. *"Where are you drawing inspiration from? You've never really been in love, have you?"*

She rarely doubted herself once she committed to something, but her dating track record made her hesitant. In 2017, Viv had been engaged and fully committed to being a one-woman woman for the rest of her life. While Viv grew up admiring her parents and aspiring to have the same love they'd found, she was also cognizant of the fact that same-sex marriage was still illegal. After 2015's landmark ruling, and queers across the country celebrated, Viv's brain was dominated by the scarcity mindset. *All of the good women are going to get snatched up and hitched. What have I been doing this whole time?*

***

Alana Ulva was the art director at a local AR/VR gaming company. She originally met Viv in late 2014, when Viv started toying with the idea of integrating augmented and virtual reality into her gallery and shows.

Viv entered their offices with her usual boisterous personality, lighting up the space. She was dressed in her typical Viv fuck-it fashion style—brown boots; skinny, light-denim jeans; a nondescript white tank, which inevitably always had paint stains on it; a reddish-brown trench coat she preferred to pin around her neck as a cape; polarized sunglasses with silver lenses; and her curly brown hair in a bun. From behind her sunglasses, she marveled at the case studies Alana's company displayed in the foyer of their offices. Although Viv's specialty was paint, she approached all other art forms with the same wonderment as the average fan—out of curiosity and a desire to learn more.

Per usual, all eyes were always on Viv, but no one's were more glued to Viv than Alana's. She had been to several of Viv's shows, but had never mustered the courage to approach her. Truth be told, she couldn't get close enough, even if she'd tried. Viv was always surrounded by a mob of women or buyers at the after-parties. As eager as she was, there was always someone more eager to get a few seconds of face time with Viv. Naturally, her excitement went through the roof when she heard that her manager had charmed Viv into taking a tour of their facility and had tapped her to lead their presentation. She worked long hours, nights, and weekends to put together a presentation to which Viv had no choice but to say yes.

Alana was particularly easy on the eyes. Brazilian descent, athletic build, five foot six with caramel-colored hair that reached her back, and piercing, greenish-gray eyes. For the meeting, she wore red lipstick, matching heels, and a formfitting, off-white dress.

She greeted Viv with a delicate handshake while trying not to blush. The Viv in front of her was different from the one she'd seen previously; this Viv was serious.

As flirtatious as Viv was known to be, when she was focused on her art, nothing else mattered. Viv soaked up the presentation Alana had apparently slaved over, creating a more immersive world for Viv's permanent gallery, gift shop, and eventually the arena, so the main space could be utilized even when Viv was traveling. There were interactive displays, apps that brought the still art to life, and a VR environment that created a simulated world where people could paint as if they were flying in the arena themselves. It was bigger, bolder, and better. Just what Viv wanted. Once the meeting was over, she instructed Gabby to sign the necessary contracts and cancel their meetings with other studios.

For weeks, Alana and Viv met one-on-one to review the proposal's progress. Viv obsessively pored over the mock-ups, wanting to understand every element. She'd ask Alana what certain words meant, so she could get better at communicating with the proper verbiage. They'd often digress into the mechanics and history behind certain elements when Viv became captivated by a detail. Alana was entertained by the process as she loved teaching, almost as much as she loved spending time with Viv.

Weekly meetings were soon downgraded to monthly meetings as they hit their stride, but Alana found reasons to see Viv more frequently. She'd take small items out of Viv's bag when Viv excused herself to go to the bathroom, just to be able to meet up after work to return them. Alana would suggest they grab a drink to unwind from their respective days, which Viv typically agreed to if she didn't already have a date planned. Eventually, Viv's phone would light up, and she'd thank Alana for her company before quickly paying the bill and heading to meet up with another woman.

Alana wondered what she could be doing wrong. A new VR show would open at the MOMA, and she'd invite Viv to the preopening festivities, even though Viv arguably had more pull than she did. Viv rarely turned any of her invitations down. She appreciated the efforts.

Finally, someone with initiative.

Still, despite all the time they'd spent together, Viv *only* wanted to talk about the work. She never wanted to talk about her personal life and didn't seem to pick up on the signals Alana was sending.

Alana's frustration grew with each passing week. She was tired of wondering why Viv hadn't made a move. She'd never had to work this hard to get anyone's attention. Man or woman. Here she was, a bombshell in her own right, months into spending time with the biggest female lothario in town, and she had zero to show for it. Had she lost her edge? Or was Viv truly not interested?

After months of meetings and prototyping, they held a beta test for the first iteration of the immersive experience. They started small with the gift shop where prints of Viv's work and other branded items could be bought. On principle, Viv hated the idea of printed replicas of her art being sold, but also understood that accessible art is the most important art.

Viv, Alana, and Alana's team watched and took notes as they tested the tech. Using the mobile beta app, testers positioned their phones over various prints. They watched the brushstrokes come to life, moving and shifting to create brand-new images. Again they shifted and expanded, showing never-before-seen snippets of Viv's process, her younger years, and her journey as an artist. Each tester's eyes lit up with excitement.

Viv was only required to stay through the testing, but she elected to stay through the entire feedback process, which took over two hours. She listened intently to each question, comment, and observation. Her mind was already iterating on what they could try next. While packing up and thanking all the testers, she informed her gallery manager to head home for the night. She'd close up shop. Viv asked Alana to stay behind to hear her latest and greatest thoughts. Her excitement was oozing out of her pores.

"Uggghhhh, that was sooooo satisfying, don't you think?" Viv asked, smiling while stretching her arms.

Alana raised her eyebrows and nodded silently.

Viv, pacing back and forth, continued, "I mean, when I create my own vision for each show, it is a once-in-a-lifetime moment that I can't recreate, but THIS…this can create so many more moments. I just… Wow. My dad's going to lose his mind when I tell him about today. I can't thank you enough for making this a reality," she said, still smiling as she placed both hands on Alana's shoulders, shaking her slightly, before dropping them back by her sides.

"Yeah, you're welcome. You'll be richer than ever once these are in production," Alana replied flatly, "and you'll actually be a contemporary artist instead of resting on your laurels with your typical circus routine."

"What? I thought you understood the vision of my work." Viv was becoming self-conscious.

"I do. I love it. You know I think you're a visionary."

"So what are you talking about?"

"Do you think I'm attractive?" Alana blurted out.

Viv's facial expression shifted from self-conscious to confusion. "What?"

Alana restated the question, "Do. You. Vivienne. Think. I, Alana. Am. Attractive? Yes or no? It's a simple question."

Viv turned and took a few steps away. She was a bit taken aback. No woman had ever been so bold towards her. She grabbed the back of her neck as she spoke, "Of course, you are. You're beautiful."

Alana was even more confused and annoyed. "So what's the problem? I'm attractive, we spend all this time together for the past six months, but you haven't responded to any of the hints I've been dropping, taken me on a date, or even bothered to eye fuck me."

"Oh, I've definitely eye fucked you when you weren't looking. But it's like you said, we've spent all this time *working* together. Professionally." Viv paused, pressing her lips together. "Gabby would kill me if she knew I fucked one of our contractors. *Again.* I almost got into some hot water with this once when I was just starting out. I didn't understand the consequences, even when it's consensual. I can't stray outside the margins without her permission. Her career and mine are intertwined at this point, and I don't want to ruin either of them. I'm sorry if that made you feel unattractive or undesirable. I was trying to do the right thing. The smart thing."

Alana took a step closer. "So if we had just met at a bar—"

Viv cut her off, replying confidently, "We would've fucked that first night. No question."

Alana took another step closer, closing the gap between them to less than a few inches. "How hard is it to get Gabby's permission?"

Viv's heart started to race, and she avoided eye contact. "Ahh, hmmm…something about consent paperwork and an ND—"

Alana grabbed Viv's hand and placed it between her legs. "Is it harder than I'm wet?" She let out a gasp, feeling Viv's fingers against her.

Viv inhaled sharply, feeling Alana's wetness. She made eye contact and shook her head no as she felt Alana's lips against hers. Softly at first. Then much more forcefully and passionately. Playtime was over. Viv pulled Alana closer, gripping her back with one hand and cupping her ass with the other. She placed her tongue at the top of Alana's cleavage and licked up her chest and her neck. Alana responded by wrapping one leg around Viv's waist and throwing her head back in ecstasy.

Viv leaned Alana against the checkout counter, unzipped Alana's dress, and dropped to her knees to help her step out of both the dress and the underwear she grabbed on the way down. Before Alana could regain her footing properly, she felt Viv's hot, eager tongue against her equally eager pussy. Alana's moans bounced off the walls of the empty studio.

Viv had imagined what Alana tasted like too many times to count, and the real thing didn't disappoint. Viv explored every fold and every crevice, first with long, slow strokes of her tongue, then followed by sucking pointedly and forcefully on her swollen clit.

Alana's hands were deep into Viv's hair, pulling her in even closer. Viv nudged her legs a little bit wider and placed them over her shoulders before gently entering Alana with two fingers. Alana gasped as her throbbing walls wrapped around Viv's fingers. Her body shaking and convulsing, she was at Viv's mercy.

Viv wrapped her lips around Alana's clit and sucked to the same rhythm that she pumped her fingers in and out of Alana's pussy, until she felt Alana's walls tighten further around her fingers. Alana's moans grew louder as the first orgasmic wave rolled through her body. Viv slowed her pace and gently alternated between circling her clit and long, slow strokes, until a second wave hit Alana.

Viv placed Alana's wobbly legs back onto the floor, sat back on her knees, and gently grabbed Alana's arms to join her on the floor. "Worth the wait?" Viv asked, her chin covered in Alana's juices.

"Definitely," Alana said in between breaths.

They spent several hours on that studio floor, until they eventually parted ways, sharing a kiss at Alana's car. As great a night as that was, Viv knew she'd fucked up. She knew she had to tell Gabby.

Viv arrived at the studio late the next morning with a lump in her throat, ready to tell the truth. Gabby beat her to the punch. She waved papers in Viv's face.

"Can you tell me why Alana Ulva showed up here bright and early this morning to sign sexual consent and NDA forms?"

Lie, bitch, lie!

"Beeeccaaauuse we talked about it after the beta test. I told her this was your process, and we had to follow it." Viv flashed the "please believe me" smile she'd used as a kid.

Gabby smiled like a proud parent. "Look at you, finally using the head above your waist for once. Six months, huh? Must be a record. Especially with a looker like that."

With that, Alana officially entered Viv's Rolodex of women, but unlike the other women, she was the one on the hunt. She consistently reached out to Viv to get on her calendar and made dinner plans to follow their prescheduled work meetings. She always knew the right thing to say to keep Viv guessing about what her next move would be. She kept Viv on her toes.

Viv soon found herself spending more time with Alana, alternating between their respective apartments in the Mission District and Noe Valley, than she did at bars and parties. She still undoubtedly enjoyed the spice of life that other women brought into her life when she wasn't with Alana, but it was also nice to not have to be the assertive one for once. They'd been sleeping together for a few months when the Supreme Court ruling officially made same-sex marriage legal in all fifty states.

After sex one night, an idea popped into Viv's head. "In a year, if they haven't found a way to overrule this, and we're still fucking, let's get engaged. What do you think?" She'd spoken cautiously, still scarred by Prop 8, a voter-approved law that banned the legalization of same-sex marriage in San Francisco in 2008. She didn't want to get her hopes up that this law would be permanent.

Alana was smitten. "Of course. I thought you'd never ask. Well, I thought you would be more romantic about it, but you have a year to think about that." She smiled as she kissed Viv, cementing their deal.

Viv made good on her promise one year later. She'd staged an elaborate light show, complete with string orchestra, at Pier 15 on a warm fall night. It ended with the lights spelling out, "Will you marry me?"

Alana excitedly said yes.

Viv smiled as they embraced. She would finally have her penguin love.

Chapter 4

All-Nighters

Ding!

The sound of the elevator opening snapped Viv out of her daydream. She was lying flat on the floor, on her back, gassed from her latest workout. She tilted her head back to see who it was.

"Oh, goodie. You're not dead," Sylvie said flatly, stepping over Viv and heading to the bar to pour herself a drink.

"Nope, not yet," Viv said sarcastically. "What are you doing here?"

"You haven't been answering anyone's calls or texts, you haven't been to the studio, you haven't been to any of the other bars, and you missed your usual nights for picking up my clientele"—Sylvie, sipping her drink, sat down on the chaise lounge chair next to Viv—"which means *I* can't cash in on all the bets those other schmucks make on how long it's gonna take for you to find someone that catches your eye. It's bad for business."

"I'm so sorry my sexcapades have eaten into your profits. Why are you really here?" Viv said while grabbing Sylvie's outstretched hand.

"Because"—Sylvie grunted as she pulled Viv in to sit with her—"you're my oldest friend, and you're not your usual functioning-alcoholic sex vixen that I know, watch over, and have been annoyed by for the last twenty-four years. What's up, chicken butt?"

Viv cracked a faint smile at the use of their childhood slang. "I don't think I can do this show, Sylv." Viv shook her head and sighed. "What if they're all right about me?" she asked, referring to the critics. "What if I don't have *it* anymore?"

Sylvie put her drink down and grabbed Viv's face with both hands. "My friend, please don't make me say something too endearing to get through to you. You've got this. You chose to do *this* show precisely to prove that you do, in fact, still have *it*."

Viv nodded.

"Now that we have that out of the way, you stink. Go take a shower so I can tell you about the chick I picked up this week." Sylvie patted Viv on the butt as she headed towards her bathroom.

***

It was an hour before showtime when Viv finally reappeared at the studio. By that time, the general-admission line had started to form. She paused for a few selfies and signed autographs until Lorenzo spotted her. She'd texted him hours ago to not wait for her at her place. She'd elected to walk to the studio. A futile attempt to clear her head.

"Viv! There you are!" Zo grabbed Viv by the arm and ushered her through the crowd. "So sooooorry, folks. You'll have to catch Viv at the meet and greet after the show."

Once inside, Viv schmoozed a bit with her usual VIPs and big bidders who were always eager to get inside information on what she had planned for the night. Zo continued to escort her backstage to her dressing room turned office, if you could call it that. It was really three mismatched, oversized canvases, which she'd declared ruined and then screwed them together one night, placing a curtain rod with coat hooks on the fourth side and a basic desk inside.

Gabby was already waiting there for her. "Are you actively trying to give me a heart attack?"

"Depends. How close am I to succeeding?" Viv asked puckishly.

"I see your little sabbatical hasn't soured your sarcasm." She took a breath and placed her hands on Viv's shoulders. "Glad you're here, kid. Did you want to go check the arena before we open the doors?"

Viv shook her head. "Nope. Where's my go-go juice?"

Gabby looked over her shoulder. "Zo?"

"On it," Zo said, shuffling away.

Gabby put her arm around Viv. "Are you sure? We made a few tweaks, and there's still time to make some small changes if it's not too your lik—"

"Gab, it's fine. Thank you, Zo." Viv grabbed her drink from a panting Zo who had rushed back. Pineapple and tequila over ice. Viv took a sip. Refreshing and satisfying, as always. "I don't think I can obsess over this show any longer. It's time to put up or shut up."

Gabby was stunned. *Did she take a sedative? Whatever, just go with it.* She put her hands up. "Okay. I'll leave you to your juice and wardrobe."

Viv had long developed a refined aesthetic for her shows. A skin-tone bodysuit, ballet shoes, and several pairs of black-latex gloves on her hands in case she chose to paint with her fingers at some point during the show. Every show started and ended the same—Viv, alone in the center of the arena on a giant, canvas-colored trampoline, her back to the audience. It gave her space and time to get in the zone before the show started and a moment to collect her thoughts before returning to the world, as it were, after it ended.

Promptly at seven, the arena went dark as Viv took her place in the usual center mark while her production crew attached her body harness to the cable system above. Once they cleared the arena, Viv took a deep breath and gave the signal to cue the music. Blue spotlights found Viv as the sultry chords of "At Last" by Etta James played on the speakers. Viv gracefully danced over to the paint station in front of her before bouncing effortlessly into the air.

Aaaaat last, my love has come along...

Viv emoted the opening track through every inch of her body. As Gabby mentioned, the layout of the arena had shifted since Viv walked out the week prior. While the audience watched where Viv's brushstrokes were going to land next, she surveyed the locations of stairs, ledges, and paint stations. She was going to have to improvise.

To the naked eye, you couldn't tell. Viv waltzed and swung in between landings. Her crew followed her on-the-fly cues and moved her to the spaces she instructed with the smoothness that comes from working together for so long. The song continued into its final two lines when she launched herself from the ledge.

And here we are in heaven.

Viv's heels aimed at the center of the canvas. An audible gasp was heard amongst the crowd; they assumed that she was planning to crash through it. When she made contact with the canvas and her heels made a slight indent, Viv was promptly launched backwards. She used the momentum to complete a backflip as she headed towards the canvas on the opposite side of the arena.

For you are miiiiiiii-iiiiiiii-iiiiine at laaaaaaast.

Viv landed against the canvas and slid down towards the floor, the music still flowing freely and effortlessly through her limbs.

With the first song and canvas jump complete, Viv's confidence radiated. She flawlessly swept through Destiny's Child's "Dangerously in Love," rocked out to Aerosmith's "I Don't Want to Miss a Thing," and felt her energy surge for Bonnie Tyler's "Total Eclipse of the Heart." The tone shifted to a somber one as the opening keys of A Great Big World's "Say Something" began. She stirred slowly through this one, heightening the pain embedded in the lyrics. Her emoting steadily increased as she moved through her set list: Gotye's "Somebody That I Used to Know," Mariah Carey's "We Belong Together," Amy Winehouse's "Back to Black," and Eminem and Rihanna's "Love the Way You Lie."

The audience hung on to Viv's every move; some were even moved to tears. It was clear to anyone watching that Viv was telling a story. A pointed and personal one. With each passing track, Viv became more and more unrestrained. She didn't see the audience, only the canvases. She'd waited two years to debut these pieces, and they proved to be as freeing as she envisioned. No wasted space in between them. They provided space to improvise, which undoubtedly helped pull the emotions further out of her.

By the closing song, Lewis Capaldi's "Someone You Loved," Viv was gassed. She glided smoothly and elegantly through the arena, as she had at the beginning of the night. When the bridge hit, Viv did something she'd never done during her shows. She stopped painting, stood atop the eight-foot canvas, holding on to the track that supported it, and sang along to the lyrics at the top of her lungs. Though barely audible to the audience, she was clearly emotionally spent. Viv the artist had disappeared, and Viv the person was on full display. Her hands in her hair, her head swinging around in circles.

And I-I-I-I-I-I tend to close my eyes when it hurts sometimes.

I fall into your aaaaaarms.

Her arms convulsing with each word. Her fingers covered in blue and lavender paint and running over her sweat-drenched face from forehead to chin.

For now the day bleeds
Into nightfaaall,
And you're not here
To get me throoough it all.
I let my guard down,
And then you pulled the rug.
I was getting kinda used to being someone you loved.

Viv snapped back into focus as she slid down the canvas as if it were a surfboard, before springboarding diagonally to the smaller canvases, flinging paint furiously before floating ominously back to the center mark as the final notes faded. All the lights went down…with the exception of a single white spotlight on Viv.

The audience rose to their feet, roaring with applause. *This* was the Viv the world fell in love with.

Viv, panting, still with her back to the audience, went from relieved to bewildered when she heard the applause abruptly fade.

What's happening?

Before she could move, she had the unmistakable feeling of another person getting onto the arena's trampoline. She froze as she felt the Intruder come closer and then stop.

"Vivi."

Viv's spine froze. The hair on the back of her neck stood up.

"Shit," Gabby's voice came through Viv's earpiece.

"Do you know who that is?" Zo asked.

Gabby sighed. "Yep." She knew she needed to get Viv out of there before things got worse. She turned on her microphone and directed Viv, "Do something. *Anything.* Just get out of the arena."

Viv turned to face the Intruder.

The Intruder took another step towards Viv, arms partially extended.

"Fuck, I guess hug her," Gabby instructed.

Viv removed her gloves, dropping them at her feet, and took a step forward to engage in what was meant to be a fake embrace. The Intruder held Viv tightly. Viv's arms relaxed around the figure before her as she rested her face in the nape of her neck. Her hair still smelled like lavender and her skin like honey.

Gabby almost found herself caught up in the emotion, as well, before coming to her senses. "Viv, out. Now."

Viv's eyes popped open as she grabbed the Intruder's wrist, led her to the edge of the arena, let go, and disappeared backstage.

The audience, taken by the added theater, roared even louder.

Chapter 5

Pinky Caressing

Viv stormed towards Gabby with panic in her eyes once she was out of the audience's sight. "Gabby, how is this happening? How is this happening?"

"Viv, that was brilliant," Zo remarked, trying to beat back the flame surging inside of his boss.

"It really was," Gabby agreed, "but I have no idea, and I will handle this."

Viv anxiously fidgeted back and forth, unconvinced.

Gabby placed both hands on Viv's shoulders and squeezed them tight. "I promise you. I will handle it. Take a deep breath, go shower, and try to get some of that paint out of your hair."

She walked towards the bathroom in a zombie-like state and locked the door behind her. She removed her performance outfit and tossed it in the laundry basket in the corner. Once in the shower, Viv, physically exhausted, was in an emotional tailspin. She pounded the walls of the shower in frustration. She slid her back against the wall to sit on the floor of the shower, leaving streaks of paint as the water cascaded over her. She held her head in her hands. Her fingers grasped at strands of her hair as her anxiety raged.

How is this happening? This can't be happening. That was her, right? I'm not imagining this? No. I can't be. Nobody else has EVER called me Vivi. What is she doing here? In person. She could've just called. Why now? Why tonight? Why make a scene? Fuck. I hope Gabby has some damage-control magic left.

She took some deep breaths and reached for her shampoo. She draped herself in her fluffy gray towel once she finished up and half dried her hair with a blow dryer. She stared at herself in the mirror and inhaled sharply.

Never let 'em see you sweat.

Viv reemerged in a black T-shirt, skinny jeans, boots, and a navy-blue blazer. Bits of paint were still on the edges of her face and embedded in her damp brown, curly hair. The after-party was in full swing, and Gabby motioned for her to come her way. Instead, she made a beeline towards Zo, who had her postshow go-go juice ready. She grabbed it, finished it in two gulps, and handed the glass back to him. Tapping her finger on his chest, she gave him instructions. "I'm going to do this meet and greet, schmooze with the big dogs and media, and then I need you to have the car ready to go. No delays. Understood?"

Zo puffed out his chest and nodded. "You got it, Boss. Any plus-ones tonight?" He looked at Viv as if she were a little sister who needed protection, just as much as he viewed her as his boss. Anything she needed, he'd make it happen.

"No. Just me."

The formalities of being a professional artist were such an energy suck for Viv. She would normally sleepwalk through it, relying on her natural charm to amuse those who demanded her attention. Her responses were well rehearsed, but her delivery always made people feel as if they were getting the inside scoop.

Tonight, Viv's mind was buzzing, which people mistook as excitement. She breezed through the meet and greet, posing for pictures with the fifty people who'd paid extra for the opportunity. Typically, this was her favorite part of her after-party duties, but today the praise from her fans fell on deaf ears.

"You moved me to tears."

"You're my favorite artist."

"So glad to have you back, Viv."

Once she took the fiftieth photo, she quickly moved on to giving some face time to the bidders and media who kept her lights on. She nodded and smiled accordingly as the superlatives continued to shower her.

"Viv, you sly devil. Always with a trick up your sleeve!"

"Looks like I'll be adding to my Vivienne Roche collection tonight."

"You can feel the emotion oozing out of your skin. It's contagious."

Uh-huh. Yeah. Sure. Thanks. My pleasure. Anytime.

Viv was a machine through the formalities. In between every smile and nod, she glanced around to see if the Intruder was still in the gallery. She couldn't get a good look with the swarm of people around her. Any other night, once she was through with the formalities, she'd bask in the attention, seeking out a companion for the night who stood out from everyone else. Not tonight. It was all business and only business. She shook the last hand that needed to be shaken and bolted towards the door, where on the other side Zo was waiting with the car, as promised.

"Where to, Boss?" he asked.

"TOP," Viv said impatiently, tapping her fingers on her leg.

***

"Viv! What a surprise, we normally don't see you on show nights," Ernie stated, flashing his signature grin and handlebar mustache. His grin quickly faded when he saw Viv was not her usual breezy self.

"Where is she?" Viv's voice boomed. All eyes in the bar were on her, but it didn't faze her.

"Uh…she's…she's in her office," Ernie responded wide-eyed.

Viv stormed past the bar and into the back of the house. Sylvie was sitting in her cramped office, papers everywhere, going over inventory, when Viv all but kicked the door in. "Did you know she was here?" Viv yelled.

"Viv, what the fuck? Who are you talking about?" a startled Sylvie asked.

Viv slammed her hand against the desk. "Don't play dumb with me. Did you know?"

Sylvie sighed. "Yes. I knew she was here."

"For how long?"

"Six months."

Viv's veins were bulging out of her neck. "Six months? Sylv, you've gotta be fucking kidding me. You're supposed to be my best fucking friend. How. On Earth. Could you not tell me this?"

"I'm *her* best friend too, remember?" Sylvie licked her lips, trying to lower the tension in the room. "Look, she asked me to stay out of it. She wanted to approach you on her own time. You know how she is. You can't push her. She does things when she's ready."

"Oh yeah?" Viv's eyebrows rose; she was becoming more unraveled by the second. "Did she tell you her own time would be entering the arena floor at the end of my show?"

"Shit."

"Yeah. Yeah." Viv sat down in the extra brown-wicker chair and leaned her elbow on the desk. "Where does she get off thinking that's somehow okay?"

"Ahhhhhh… Your show must've spoken to her," Sylvie said, flipping her hands in the air. "She's been to all your shows since she moved here."

"Moved? Every show? You said you knew she was here, but… moved… What even…" Viv was tripping over her words. She grabbed the bridge of her nose and shut her eyes. "You know what, Sylv? I can't continue this conversation with you right now." She stood and turned towards the door.

"You should really hear her out, Viv!" Sylvie yelled.

Viv responded by flipping the middle finger as she exited. She reentered the bar in a huff, still seeing red.

"Viv!" A voice yelled out. It was Belle, seated in Viv's usual booth. "Didn't you have a show tonight? How'd it go?"

"Great. It was great, Belle," Viv said, faking a smile.

Belle stood and seductively walked towards Viv. Grabbing Viv's bicep, she said, "You're tense. You wanna get out of here?"

"You have no idea." Viv patted Zo on the back as he sat at the end of the bar. "Take the rest of the night off, Zo. I can get myself home."

"You sure, Boss?" Zo asked with concerned eyes.

"Yes. I'm sure. I'll text you if anything changes. I promise."

Zo smiled and nodded in approval.

Once outside, Belle clicked the key fob for her Tesla Model X and gestured towards the passenger seat. "After you." As the spaceship doors of the Model X started closing, Belle slipped her hand between Viv's legs. "You *definitely* need to relax," she remarked.

They took the short two-minute drive from TOP, around the corner to Belle's condo. In theory, she could just walk there, but she refused to ruin her designer heels on the signature hills of the Bay Area. Belle's hand never moved, her pinky nudging against Viv's clit through her jeans.

Viv needed a distraction, and there was no better one in her mind than sex. Even if her head wasn't there, her body would eventually help it catch up.

As the front door closed behind them, Belle wasted no time. She removed Viv's blazer and tossed it on the couch, Viv's bra on the landing, and her shirt on the second step; then Belle carried Viv up the stairs. Once in the master bedroom, she gently pushed Viv face-first onto her king-sized bed and mounted her. She leaned in to whisper in Viv's ear, "Tonight's your night to be taken care of."

She laid kisses from Viv's neck down her back before unbuttoning and removing her jeans and underwear. Viv let out a gasp as she felt Belle's tongue running along her outer lips. Belle repeated her motion a few more times, getting a full taste as Viv's lips opened up more with each lick. With Viv warmed up to her satisfaction, Belle slowly inserted two fingers into her pussy as far as they would go, before removing them slowly and repeating.

Viv let out an audible moan, her breath getting more labored with each motion. Her hands gripped the sheets as she felt her orgasm building.

Sensing this, Belle removed her fingers and moved to plant a kiss on the back of Viv's ears. "Not yet. Just wait here for one second," Belle whispered.

Viv buried her face in a pillow while her body writhed on the bed impatiently, waiting to have the release she desperately craved. She heard muffled noises in the next room and then Belle's footsteps coming closer.

Belle ran her hand over Viv's perfectly toned ass. "I'm baaack." She pulled Viv closer to her, Viv's ass pointing up in the air.

Viv felt the unmistakable sensation of a strap-on entering her pussy. Viv leaned her ass into Belle, wanting to be filled faster.

"Gooood girl," Belle crooned. She was fully inside Viv now. "Comfortable?"

"Mmm-hmmmm," Viv said, nodding her head slightly.

Belle placed her hands on either side of Viv's hips and fucked her. Hard.

Each thrust had Viv gasping for air and moaning in approval. Each thrust took her further from the events at the gallery and deeper into the euphoric feeling of the moment. "Harder," she managed to whisper.

Belle obliged. She grabbed Viv by the shoulders, sending shock waves further into Viv's nerve endings. She took her right hand and sucked on two fingers before reaching around Viv to circle her clit.

Viv lost it. Her body contracted, and her moans became strained as her orgasm washed over her. "Fffff…fuck-fuuuuck! Ah!" A second wave hit her as Belle continued thrusting, but at a softer, slower pace. Viv's body collapsed onto the bed, still convulsing in pleasure.

Belle laid her body on top of Viv's, moving Viv's hair to the side and kissing her neck. "Relaxed?" Belle asked.

"Mm-hmm. Very," Viv whispered, drifting to sleep as Belle held her.

Chapter 6
Subway Stations

Bzzz…Bzzz…

   Bzzz…Bzzz…

   Bzzz…Bzzz…

   Bzzz…Bzzz…

"Viv. Viv. Wake up," Belle said, shaking Viv's shoulder.

"Hmmm… What? What's going on," she said in between deep breaths, rubbing both eyes with the palms of her hands and trying to remember where she was.

"Your phone has been blowing up all morning. Here." Belle handed the phone to Viv.

Viv lay on her back and read her messages.

Gabby: Viv! When are you coming in?

Gabby: We need to talk!

Gabby: Can't wait!

Gabby: Just went by your place. What cave did you crawl into this time?

Gabby: Vivienne Elizabeth Roche. Wake your ass up.

Viv: I'm awake. What's the emergency?

Gabby: We need to talk. Get to the studio ASAP.

Viv: Ay captain. I'll share my location when I'm on the way.

Viv placed her palms on her eyes and rubbed them again. "Goddammit, I hate my life sometimes." She sighed.

"Work?" Belle asked.

Viv nodded.

"Do you want some coffee while you wait for your ride to get here?"

"Nah," Viv said, waving her hand. "I'll be fine."

"I'm sure of that. I thought you might want something to occupy your time while you wait. Oooor we could actually talk to each other," Belle said rhetorically.

True.

"Soy milk, two sugars, please."

Belle smiled and headed downstairs. "Sure thing."

While Viv collected her trail of clothing, she noticed, hanging in the stairwell, one of her paintings from a show she did in 2009. "How have I not noticed that before?" she asked, reaching for her cup of coffee.

"You were pretty preoccupied both times you've been here," Belle said slyly.

Viv nodded and sipped her coffee.

"Now we're even," Belle said assertively, turning in her black-lace robe and sipping her own coffee.

"What do you mean?" Viv asked.

"You know you're not the only one that believes in meaningless sex. I just can't be a kept woman. I always have to return the favor."

Viv raised her cup and gestured as if to say, "Cheers."

They continued sipping in silence until Viv's car arrived. Belle walked Viv to the door.

"Uhhhh…thanks," Viv said.

"Anytime, Viv," Belle replied, planting a quick kiss on her lips.

Inside the Lyft, Viv closed her eyes on the ride back into the city, certain that would be the last peace she had for the day.

***

At the studio, Viv arrived to Gabby's outstretched arms. "Ha! There you are." *Muaaahh!* Gabby planted a big kiss on Viv's lips.

"Gab, ew," Viv said, wiping her lips with the back of her hand.

"You'd kiss yourself too if you could! Come! Sit." Gabby motioned for Viv to join her on the couches that made up half of her open office. Her assistants were buzzing around the office already working on their revised to-do lists. "Look at this! We're back, baby!" she said, punching the air and sliding in front of Viv the reviews from several newspapers and blogs.

All of the reviews were glowing.

Not since Geraldine and Henri have we seen such brilliance!

Vivienne Roche, the master emoter, strikes gold again.

You had to be there to understand the ethereality of the moment.

Using her patented canvas tech, she flew like an angel...

A mystery woman appeared to strike a chord with our resident lothario...

She disappeared as quickly as she appeared...

Artistic theater or a serendipitous reunion? The world wants to know. Who is this woman?

***

Ryan Pearce was born in White Plains, New York, to a conservative military family. Her dad, Jack, had fought in the Vietnam War. He received a Purple Heart and an honorable discharge from the army after he was shot in his left knee by a sniper. Her mom, Mayu—or May, as Jack called her—was a Japanese immigrant and a nurse. She cared for Jack at the James J. Peters Department of Veterans Affairs Medical Center in the Bronx when he returned to the States.

Jack, used to being a physical specimen at six foot four and 235 pounds, was reduced to barely more than an infant during his hospital stay. He'd bark at every nurse and doctor who saw him. May was the only one to whom he'd listen, but not before learning the hard way. He'd insisted that he could walk on his own and demanded that his restraints be removed so he could get up and show her.

"Fine," she said curtly one day, "show me." She removed his wrist restraints, lowered the guardrail, and took a few steps back, arms crossed.

He stared back at her with a pompous smirk on his face. He swung his legs across the bed to the right and sat up with both fists pressed against the mattress. "Watch me." He grinned with raised eyebrows. He hopped onto the floor and instantly crumpled in pain, grabbing at his knee. "Aaaarrrrgghh. God! Damn it!"

May, chuckling at the sight of his antics, covered her mouth to try and hide her amusement. "God has nothing to do with you thinking you are Superman, you big dummy."

Wincing in pain, he scooched himself closer to his bed. "Will ya help me, or are ya just gonna stand there laughin'?"

"*Now* you want my help?" she replied, enjoying that she'd brought this big man down to size.

"Yes," he said meekly, his hand outstretched in her direction.

"You don't have manners?" She lowered her brow at him, waiting to see if he'd say the magic words.

Jack rolled his eyes and sighed. "Yes, please, Mayu."

She knelt beside him and put her right arm around him before lifting him back up onto the bed. He let out a painful sigh of relief as she put his knee back in the sling that hung from the ceiling. "There you go. Good as new," she said, smoothing out his bushy eyebrows and lightly petting his thick brown hair. "And you can call me May," she added with a smile before turning to leave.

"May? Hold on."

"Yes, Jack?" she said, turning around.

"You can be the boss in here. But out there"—he paused, pointing at the window—"out there, I'm the boss."

"Hmmmm, we'll see." They shared a smile before she went to the next room.

Jack courted May throughout his rehabilitation, and they were married a few short months later. They moved to White Plains, which offered a better environment than New York City for raising a family. It was an easy-enough commute for May to get to the Bronx, while Jack started a real estate investing company with a friend and volunteered at the local Army Recruiting Office. May softened Jack's sharp edges and made him more enjoyable to everyone who knew him.

Unfortunately, Ryan never got to meet that version of Jack, nor was her childhood half as colorful as Viv's. May died while giving birth to her, a sin for which Jack never forgave Ryan. Truthfully, he resented both Ryan and May the moment he found out they were having a daughter instead of a second son. May assured him that he would change his mind once he met baby Josephine, the name May had picked out, and promised him that she would make them both proud when she grew up.

The first few weeks after Ryan's birth, he'd have his buddies over for drinks while he reluctantly bounced his new daughter on his knee. They'd all comment on what a beautiful baby girl she was, but May's death was seen as karma for Jack's marrying "a no good Jap." Between his grief and his friends' commentary, he would go on to believe that had he married an American woman, she would've survived the complications May suffered during delivery.

Jack chose to do the bare minimum for Ryan and poured all of his energy into their firstborn child, Jack Jr., who was three years her elder. Junior was a clone of their father—tall, lean, bushy eyebrows, and an obsession for the military. When they were kids, Junior would often beg for Ryan to be included in their activities, much to the annoyance of Jack. When he begrudgingly agreed, Junior would smile and pat her on the chest. "Okay, Ry, come on! You have to keep up!"

Ryan gleefully ran behind them. Despite Junior's best efforts, she was eventually banned from joining any of their activities when she was nine, after she squealed during a hunting trip and scared away a rabbit.

Junior was less sexist than his father, but could only act as a buffer between them as Jack chose to live a life that didn't include Ryan. While she spent her afternoons playing with dolls donated by neighbors, Jack put Junior through basic-training drills. She spent her nights sketching fashion designs while they played Grand Theft Auto or Active Shooter video games. Until Halo came out. Then it was all about Halo.

At school, Ryan was often the only mixed-race girl and certainly the only hapa haole. Junior got a pass because he was popular. Plus, Jack, who bragged about him at every turn, was well respected in the community. Ryan was more of a mystery since he rarely spoke of her. Despite having her spirit boxed in at home, she had a personality that blossomed when anyone interacted with her elsewhere. She excelled in academics, and her warm personality and fashion sense allowed for inroads to be made with a few of the more popular girls.

One of her teachers, Mrs. Dolton, took note of her fashion-design talents and encouraged her to think bigger than her sketchbook. Ryan's mother had had a successful side business as a tailor and seamstress, and she'd clearly passed it on to her daughter. Ryan had a talent that couldn't be taught, and it flowed through her fingers onto the page. Mrs. Dolton secured her a spot in an after-school fashion program. There she could hone her design skills, learn how to sew, and build a portfolio for university applications.

Her early work impressed everyone around her. Except Jack. His world remained all about Junior. He attended every single one of Junior's JROTC exhibitions, but never thought to ask when Ryan's were or even knew they were happening. One evening, when Jack bothered to notice she wasn't home, upon her arrival, he inquired as to her whereabouts.

Her eyes lit up, elated that her father was giving her attention. She proudly said, "At my fashion show! I wo—"

"Fucking girls," Jack cut her off abruptly and walked away.

Ryan should've been used to being dismissed and ignored by now, but she wasn't. She somberly walked to her room and put her first-place ribbon next to all the others on her shelf. She sat on the floral comforter that draped her twin bed and counted the days until she'd graduate high school.

Her fifteenth birthday, July 16, 2000, was the proudest day of Jack's life. It was the day Junior shipped out for basic training. With Junior out of the house, Jack's behavior remained unchanged. He'd give Ryan money to do "womanly duties," like grocery shopping, but he never provided much of a budget for back-to-school shopping. As a result, Ryan made most of her clothes, providing further education on how to properly construct a garment.

Their home became much more unbearable now that her buffer was gone. Junior was no longer around to talk to at home, and Jack could barely look at her. As she matured, she became more of a spitting image of her mother with each passing day. It was a reality that forced the resurfacing of Jack's grief about May's death and stoked his hatred of Ryan.

Things would only get worse. Two years later, on April 18, 2002, Junior was sent to Afghanistan and was killed in combat six short weeks later. Jack's world crumbled. When they shipped his body back for the funeral, it was the only time she ever saw an ounce of vulnerability from Jack. His depression from the loss of his "only child" deepened his resentment toward Ryan.

With what little time she spent at home, Ryan either sketched or dreamed of the day she'd start college. Mrs. Dolton stepped up when Jack refused to pay for her application fees.

The second proudest day of Jack's life was on August 9, 2003, when after Ryan moved herself into the dorms at Parsons School of Design in New York City, Jack acknowledged that he'd survived eighteen years with Ryan.

***

"White mocha with soy! White mocha with soy!" The barista at the cafe on campus placed the drink on the counter.

Viv reached for her drink and bumped hands with another student. "Oh, I'm sorry. Is that yours? I wasn't paying attention," she said, pulling off her headphones. Viv had been lost in thought, ignoring the students buzzing around the cafeteria. She'd only turned her music down just enough to hear her order called.

"Yeah. I mean, I think so. I don't know who got here first. Did you order the same?" the stranger asked.

"Yep."

"Great minds think alike." The stranger smiled, staring down at the floor.

"They do." Viv scratched the back of her neck, suddenly speechless. She was taken by the sight in front of her. This stranger, with equally superior coffee taste, was stunning. She stood around five foot six and had dark-brown eyes. Viv deduced that she was definitely mixed race from her coloring—slightly olive-toned skin and long, wavy, dark-brown, almost-black hair that reached the middle of her back. She had a colorful tattoo sleeve with symbols of the Japanese religion Shinto interwoven with roses that tucked underneath the burnt-orange top she was wearing. "Um, you can have that one. I can wait."

"You sure? That's killer, thanks! I'm running late for class anyway. See you around." She smiled, walked out of the cafe, and passed Sylvie. "Oh hey, Sylvie! Gotta run."

Viv made a beeline towards her best friend. "Sylvie, Sylvie, Sylvie! Who's that?" she asked incessantly, rapidly tapping Sylvie on the shoulder.

"Oh, that's Ryan. Fashion major. Supposed to be hot shit." Sylvie shrugged while she ordered a coffee.

Viv's eyes widened. "How do YOU know her, and I don't?"

"I had drawing class with her last semester," Sylvie replied, walking around to the pickup counter. "She can draw her ass off, no lie."

"She gay?" Viv asked, following Sylvie.

"No." Sylvie scoffed. "Why do you care?"

"Because," Viv said, her eyes lighting up, "I felt the spark."

Sylvie rolled her eyes and threw her head back. "Ugh, you and this spark bullshit. I keep telling you our lives aren't like your parents. They're hyperfunctional, super in love, and happily married. You know how many other couples I know like that? Zilch. Zero. Nada. Nulla. Nought."

"Yeah, yeah, I get it." Viv waved her off, staring in the direction that Ryan had walked.

Sylvie continued, "You date these girls for two or three weeks and give up because you don't feel a spark or it wasn't sparky enough. Now you expect me to believe you felt it with some *straight* girl?"

"White mocha with soy! White mocha with soy!" Viv's drink was ready.

"The spark thing is real, and I'm telling you, Sylv, I felt it," Viv said, grabbing her drink.

"And I'm telling you she's S-T-R-A-I-G-H-T. Straight, Viv. Get it through your thick head."

"Whatever. Who does she hang out with?" Viv asked, undeterred.

"I don't really know. Fashion people, I guess. She invited me to some NYU party her friends are throwing this weekend or something." Sylvie had grown bored with the conversation.

"Great. We're going." Viv patted Sylvie on the shoulder.

Sylvie sighed.

"Love exists my friend!" Viv said triumphantly, pointing at the sky as she exited the cafe. "You just have to have a little faith."

***

Viv slammed the reviews down on the table. "Gabby, this is bullshit. After all of our work on this show, all of these articles end on this huge piece around who she is and what her backstory could be. She upstaged me at my own show!" She hunched over with her elbows on her knees, resting her head in her right hand. She lightly massaged her temples as if she could will her nightmare away.

"*Exactly!*" Gabby pumped both fists at Viv. "My phone, email, you name it, has been going nuts since you left last night. We need to ride this wave while we've got it." Gabby was a shark in her own right—always on the ball, forever an opportunist, and endlessly seizing the moment.

It was the same attitude that had made Viv into a household name. It also gave Viv fits and at times made her feel powerless about the trajectory of her career. "What does that exactly mean, Gab?" Viv asked, still barely awake and tightly holding her eyes closed.

"Wel—"

"Hate to interrupt." It was Zo. "The car with Ms. Pearce just pulled up."

For a brief moment, Viv blacked out.

Chapter 7

Diesel

"We're here with Kelly!" Sylvie yelled over the music coming out of the house where the unofficial Kappa Gamma party was raging. A fire truck whizzed by on the street behind them.

"Okay, cool!" The blonde-haired girl with a bright-pink face at the door seemed ambivalent to whether or not that was the truth.

"Is that the person we're looking for?" Viv asked as she followed Sylvie into the party.

Sylvie scrunched up her face and shrugged. "I have no idea, but there's always someone named Kelly at a sorority party."

They weaved their way through the house, Sylvie searching for the drink table and Viv scanning the room for Ryan. The place, like every college party, was crawling with people. There was a group playing beer pong in the corner, stoners smoking weed on the fire escape, and horny freshmen grinding on each other to the latest crunk music. Viv spotted a few girls in the middle of a three-way kiss, which caught her attention, causing her to temporarily stop her search.

"No way, Viv." Sylvie grabbed Viv's arm. "You don't want those girls."

"Why not?"

Sylvie pointed in their direction. "Those are just spaghetti girls."

Viv looked confused.

Sylvie, gesturing with her hands, decoded the statement, "Straight until wet. Come on. I think I just heard someone say there were Jell-O shots in the kitchen."

They squeezed their way into the kitchen to find both the Jell-O shots…and Ryan. Sylvie gave her a side hug. "Hey, hey, Ry! How's it goin'? Thanks for inviting me. You remember my friend Viv, yeah?"

Ryan, clearly tipsy already, pointed at Viv and squinted with one eye. "Coffee shop, right?"

"Yep. That was…that was me." Viv, awestruck again by Ryan's presence, was unable to utter anything more.

Ryan wore a sleeveless black jumpsuit that hugged her body perfectly, a small white belt around her waist. Her face had turned bright red after the first couple of drinks that night. "Oh gosh! You were a lifesaver that day. I'm always running late somehow. These are my friends Cara, Tracy, and Steph. They go to NYU."

Viv and Sylvie waved politely.

"Here! Do a Jell-O shot with us," Ryan said, handing them cherry-flavored shots.

"Cheeeeeers!" they all said in unison as they downed the alcohol-infused gelatin.

At that moment, "Get Low" by Lil Jon and the East Side Boyz started playing, and the kitchen cleared out as they all rushed to the dance floor. The rest of the night was mostly a blur to Ryan.

She vaguely remembered dancing, drinking, doing shots, and dancing some more. Wash, rinse, repeat. The air-conditioning unit in the window barely made a difference in the packed living room. The heat was the one thing she could remember. She felt her blood pumping through her body as the temperature and her alcohol intake rose.

For Viv, the night was crystal clear. She was captivated by Ryan's every move. The way she held her hair back while she danced as if no one were watching. The effusiveness with which she greeted all of her friends. Her drunken joy was spanning ear to ear with every sip of alcohol. When she wasn't dancing herself, Viv would find a space on the wall to lean against and casually watch in awe as she sipped on her drink.

Lightweights.

Growing up sipping wine in the back of art galleries, she learned how to pace herself and what her limits were at an early age. Despite swearing off alcohol in elementary school, it shifted from a disgusting experiment to a source of quiet comfort in high school. It dampened her anxiety, which provided her greater focus on her work.

Sylvie broke Viv's trance, leaning her sweaty face into her ear. "I think I'm gonna go get a Hot Pocket!" she yelled over the music.

That was their code for "I'm gonna leave and go hook up with someone. You're on your own."

Viv nodded, wiping Sylvie's sweat off her face. "Enjoy."

"Cool, don't wait up." Sylvie brushed her way towards the exit.

Viv adjusted her focus to try and find Ryan in the crowd. Watching adults at gallery parties over the years had also taught her how to spot when someone had had too much. All too often someone had to be escorted out of a gallery or could hilariously be seen arguing with the art itself. This party was full of those people.

She noticed Ryan come out of the bathroom, stand in the doorway, and steady herself with her hands against the frame before stumbling forward a few steps. "Are you okay?" Viv intervened, grabbing Ryan's arm before she fell. "Where are your friends?"

"Mmmmmm…I'm not exactly sure. Maaaybbeee…over there!" Ryan pointed emphatically, drunkenly, and incorrectly.

"Okay. Stay right here. I'll see if I can find them," Viv said, making Ryan sit on the couch next to the stoners. She searched upstairs, downstairs, the front steps, and the fire escape, but to no avail. She returned to see that, thankfully, Ryan hadn't moved. Primarily because she had fallen asleep. "Hey. Hey, Ryan." Viv lightly tapped her face to wake her. "I can't find your friends. What's your address so I can take you home?"

Ryan mumbled a string of incoherent words that didn't help answer the question.

"Do you have your own place? Are you staying in Loeb? You know, the brick building with the planters on the front patio?"

Ryan responded with more words that ultimately left Viv with no option.

Guess you're comin' home with me then. Viv grabbed Ryan's arm and draped it over her neck to lift her off the couch. They slowly walked four long city blocks east to Viv and Sylvie's apartment on Second Avenue and East Twelfth. Viv had one hand securely around Ryan's waist and the other keeping Ryan's arm draped over her neck. She stared off into the night silently while they walked.

"Ooh!" Ryan interjected. "Is it raining?" she asked.

"No. That's just an air-conditioning unit dripping on you," Viv responded flatly.

Ryan jumped at the sound of twenty or so dirt bikes racing down Third Avenue.

Viv held her a little tighter at the waist, "It's okay. I've got you."

"Ugh! Is it raining again?"

Viv smiled and shook her head. "No, Ry, that's just another air-conditioning unit."

"Ooooh, yeaaaah. You told me that already!" Ryan laughed, throwing her head onto Viv's collarbone.

Through the smell of alcohol, Viv became entangled by the lavender scent of Ryan's hair as it brushed against her face. They continued to walk in silence.

"You're very pretty," Ryan mumbled while staring at the sidewalk.

Viv's cheeks were flush with heat. "Thank you."

***

Where the fuck am I?

Ryan awoke the next morning with a pounding in her head that was inevitable after consuming three drinks made with cheap alcohol and five shots on an empty stomach. Unfamiliar with her surroundings, she sat up and rubbed her eyes, working to collect her thoughts. She attempted to piece together what she was seeing as she sat up on the brown-leather couch, the taste of vodka still on her tongue. The sun beamed in through large loftlike windows onto unfinished paintings on easels, material clippings, and mood boards just past the couch and empty beer bottles and pizza boxes on the coffee table in front of her.

"Morning, sleepyhead." Smiling, Viv appeared from the kitchen behind Ryan. "Here's some chamomile tea to soothe your insides, saltine crackers, if you can eat them, to build up the sodium that alcohol extracts from your body, and Motrin Extra Strength for your head." Viv placed her morning care package at the edge of the coffee table.

"Ugh, thank you. I drank waaay too much last night," Ryan replied, reaching for the dark-blue mug.

"No sweat. Happens to the best of us." Viv avoided eye contact as she grabbed some of the pizza boxes and beer bottles off the coffee table and walked towards the kitchen.

Ryan followed with her eyes. "Thanks for not ditching me at the party...like my friends clearly did."

"No biggie. Sorry about the mess in here. I wasn't really expecting company." Viv returned to the living room with her own cup of tea in hand and sat, with one knee bent, in the maroon accent chair.

Ryan nervously leaned in her direction and whispered, "Did we...you know...do *it* last night?"

Viv smiled, trying to hide her own nerves. "We did not."

Ryan sighed in relief. "Oh…okay. Well, thanks again. I can get my shit together and get out of your hair. I'm sure you have tons of things you want to do today without a stranger in your apartment."

"No, no, it's okay. Take your time. I was just going to work on some of this chaos sitting here in front of you."

"Is this yours?" Ryan asked, pointing to the material board.

"No, that's Sylvie's. She's in interiors. I'm in fine arts. This is mine," Viv replied while pointing to her canvas.

Ryan curiously surveyed the canvases before spinning her head back towards Viv. "Maybe you can tell me more about it after I have more tea?"

"Sounds good."

Ryan spent the morning lying on the couch, sipping tea, and watching Viv work in silence while wearing headphones. She marveled at the way Viv behaved when she was locked in the zone. She'd stand back and stare at her work, poke her lip with the back of her paintbrush, and then reengage with a manic fervor, oscillating between focusing on tiny details and broad brushstrokes. Eventually, she found a good stopping point and ordered lunch for the two of them.

They spent the afternoon on the couch, laughing and chatting about their favorite artists while they ate dim sum. Ryan used Viv's computer to show off her digital portfolio, which contained sketches and photos from her high school fashion shows. Ryan would playfully laugh at Viv's word choices when she asked questions about the details of her designs.

"I like this shaky stuff." Viv made her wrist go limp and shook it side to side to illustrate.

"You mean fringe?"

"Yeah, that! And this one"—Viv pointed to a different detail—"the, um, crunchy part."

"You mean pleated?"

Viv pointed excitedly in Ryan's direction. "Yes, exactly! That word!"

Ryan laughed uncontrollably. "How do you not know these words?"

Viv laughed along, defending herself, "Hey, hey, hey! I'm a painter. Not a fashion designer. I can't know everything. That would just be unfair to the rest of you." She puffed her chest out and pointed her nose in the air.

"Well, aren't you so gracious?" Ryan replied sarcastically, clutching her invisible pearls.

The conversation between them flowed effortlessly, as if they'd known each other their whole lives, instead of having had just two chance encounters. Hours passed without either of them noticing. There was never a prolonged silence or uncomfortable moment, until Sylvie returned from her nightly conquest.

Sylvie's eyes lit up when she saw Ryan and Viv sitting cozily together. "Holy shit, did you guys fuck?" She leaned against the door.

Viv bugged her eyes out at her forward friend. "Sylv!"

"What? It's a fair question." Sylvie shrugged, undeterred by the notion.

Viv dropped her head in her hands in embarrassment. "No, dude. Damn." A palpable tension could be felt in the room.

"Uh, I really should get going. I still smell like last night," Ryan interjected, quickly gathering her things. "Thanks again, Vivi. We should hang out again sometime. See ya, Sylvie." She scooted herself behind Sylvie to quickly open the door and squeeze through.

As the door closed, Sylvie raised her eyebrows with an amused grin on her face. "Vivi?"

"Fuck off."

***

From that day on, they were the three amigas. They spent all of their free time together outside of class and the studio. They would critique each other's work, which in turn challenged them all to be better. Socially, they owned the night. Viv and Sylvie taught Ryan how to handle her liquor, and Ryan introduced them to cigarettes. They were each other's wingwomen at night and gave each other shit for their choices in the days that followed. Except for Ryan.

She was happy to go out and socialize, but didn't want to be bothered with dating or flirting. She seemed content to watch Sylvie and Viv work their magic. The nights were electric across the Lower East Side. They'd walk up and down Saint Mark's Place, which was bustling with college students and young artists. It was a bit of an obstacle course as every other door had people spilling in and out of restaurants and bars. They'd hit up Empanada Mama's and load up on three-dollar *empanadas* before raging.

Viv and Sylvie where cognizant of the need to frequent an equal number of gay and straight bars, in case Ryan wanted to find someone in whom she was interested. But she never was. When they asked why, she said that she'd tried dating in her first semester, but it was too difficult to keep up with her work and maintain a budding relationship. It was hard to argue with that.

Ryan was the hot-shot freshman, and she worked hard to keep up her reputation. Inside, she never felt a connection with the guys who liked her. It was either they weren't mentally stimulating enough for her, or she'd find out that they fetishized her being half Japanese, which was an instant turnoff.

Watching Viv and Sylvie was similar to watching a sitcom. A *telenovela* may be more apropos since it was a nightly affair. It didn't matter in what room they were; their personas would light up any space into which they walked. Ryan often wondered how they knew if a girl they were talking to was gay or not. Their secret? They didn't care. They were unapologetically themselves one hundred percent of the time. That authenticity made it easy for them to attract and successfully bed the women they met.

Ryan's personality grew in the months that they spent together. Initially, she was extremely reserved, but they pushed her to live her life out loud. "Fuck the haters!" That was their mantra. Ryan's confidence began to shine brighter than it ever had, but she still felt as if something was missing. She felt she'd found her chosen family in Viv and Sylvie, but despite that, she still felt like an outsider. When she looked at them, she wanted to *be* them. But was that possible?

The parties faded to a trickle as finals approached. Viv intently painted in the living room, Sylvie was in her studio making models of her designs, and Ryan locked herself in the fashion studio amongst the hundreds of mannequins and tables for cutting patterns. Their conversations were held mostly by text, late into the night once they'd worked themselves into the ground for the day.

After finals, they went out for celebratory drinks on the rooftop of the Gansevoort Hotel in the Meatpacking District. It was fancy for them, but they felt the need to splurge after a long first year. As they reflected on the year and how they'd come to know each other, the conversation shifted to next fall.

"You know, Viv, as much as I *sort of* enjoy your company, I'm not going to miss coordinating my hookups with yours," Sylvie said as she leaned on the glass balcony, taking in the view of the West Side.

"What do you mean?" Ryan had been out of the loop on certain conversations since she had little time to come over during finals.

"She's getting her own place," Viv said.

Ryan looked surprised. "You are? Why?"

Sylvie laughed. "Viv's tired of losing women to me."

Viv playfully shoved Sylvie. "It was once in eleventh grade!"

"Ha, see? It still riles her up. For real, though, my uncle just confirmed that he's moving back to LA to open his firm's new law office. Apparently, divorces are booming over there. He's going to rent his condo to me at the favorite-niece rate. Gonna move my stuff into storage until I come back. So it's *sayonara*, suckers! Ya girl's movin' on up! I'm gonna own the West Side!" She stretched her arms out over the balcony.

Ryan turned to Viv. "What about you, Vivi?"

Viv shrugged and stared out across the balcony. "Gotta find a roommate, and hopefully convince my parents we can afford it if I don't."

"What if I moved in?" Ryan offered. "I'm kinda over living in the dorms, and my professor offered me a summer internship if I could find a place to stay."

Viv's heart fluttered at the thought of getting to see Ryan every night and every morning. Sure, they'd become best friends over the semester, but Viv still had a crush. "Yeah! That would be great. I know we all hang out there anyway, but I didn't want to assume that you'd want to."

"Great! Roomies it is!" Ryan beamed, pulling Viv in for a hug.

Sylvie turned in the opposite direction to roll her eyes. Her best friend was a glutton for punishment.

Chapter 8

Farmers Markets

The summer couldn't pass fast enough. While Viv still relished every moment back home, she couldn't wait to return to New York. She'd spend her typical days at her mom's gallery, just as she did growing up, helping to curate and coordinate her mother's upcoming shows. In the early evening, Viv painted in their studio to clear her head, and she played games with her parents late into the night. She still genuinely loved playing board games, card games, and Taboo with them, as they were all fiercely competitive, but a small part of her was always distracted.

Every second that she had, she'd be glued to her phone in a group chat with Sylvie and Ryan or on a one-on-one thread with just Ryan. Sharing updates of their lives and inside jokes, grappling with the growing pains of transitioning back home after having a year of freedom. Ryan, electing to stay in the city, continued to exercise her freedom. She was enjoying the summer weather and attending the various rooftop parties with friends, but it wasn't the same without her partners in crime.

With Sylvie, Viv excitedly returned to New York in early August. Well, sort of. During the summer, Sylvie had randomly met a girl at a BART station. Her name was Jennifer, she went to Fordham in the Bronx, and they'd become virtually inseparable all summer. Jen's family had built an art gallery in Big Sur back in the day, before it became a haven for the rich. Her dad was an artist as well, and the land they owned was now worth millions of dollars. Jen effectively and self-professedly attended college for shits and giggles. With all their pet names and pillow talk, Sylvie and Jen might as well have been sniffing each other's butts on the plane. Though Jen was the type of silver-spoon kid she loathed, Viv was unbothered. Her mind was solely on seeing Ryan again.

They split a cab from JFK, with Viv getting dropped off first, before Sylvie and Jen continued on to the West Side. Excited as she was to be back, it was this part Viv hated. With sweat dripping down her neck, she lugged her suitcase up three flights of stairs, full of stagnant humid air, to return to her apartment, or what she thought was her apartment.

When she lived with Sylvie, they were borderline frat boys with the way they lived day to day. Dishes and pizza boxes would pile up until one of them got fed up and cleared the mess, only for it to return by the next weekend. Glasses and utensils were never one hundred percent clean, and they microwaved everything. Their personal projects overflowed onto each other, and at times it felt as if they were working on top of one another. It was never filthy, but it was always a chaotic mess.

The apartment that Viv walked into was sparkling clean. Brighter even. The windows had been cleaned for the first time in…ever? There were magazines neatly lying across the coffee table. As if real adults lived there. There was a new black, high-top table set in the kitchen and in the former dining room. There was a defined space with Viv's easel and canvases leaning against a wall. Her art supplies were neatly stored in a contemporary bookshelf and organized by paint color and brush size. On the other side of the apartment was an area complete with two mannequins draped in different fabrics, a table, and a sewing machine.

As Viv took in the changes, she heard the sound of the front door unlocking and turned to see Ryan clumsily making her way in with bags full of groceries. She dropped them at the door when she saw Viv.

"Aaaaaaaah, you're BACK!" she screamed as she ran into Viv's arms.

"Ooof! Yeeeeeuuup, I am!" Viv grinned ear to ear while she returned the embrace. "Ry, this place…it looks amazing. I didn't even recognize it."

"I hope it wasn't too much," Ryan said, smiling nervously. "I know it was your apartment first, so we can always go back to the way it was before."

"No, no. It's great. Really," Viv said as she gave Ryan a soft squeeze on the arm.

"Great. I also cleaned your room a little." Ryan flashed another nervous smile at the admission that she'd trespassed.

"Thanks, RyRy." Viv laughed, working to hide how smitten she was, as she moved past Ryan to get settled into her "new" apartment.

***

The three amigas became two that semester. Between living on the West Side and spending her free time in the Bronx with Jen, Sylvie had all but disappeared from their social circle. Meanwhile, Viv and Ryan picked up right where they left off. On their wild nights, they'd be out on the town at a rooftop party, soaking up the warm summer nights New York provided. More often than not, as they had their freshman year, those nights ended with Viv bringing someone home and Ryan in her room sketching designs, listening to music, and fervently trying to block out the sounds creeping out from the other bedroom. On their mellow nights, they'd sit on the couch, sketching together, chatting for hours, watching movies, or working in their new home studios.

One particular night, Ryan had a phone call from Mrs. Dolton that lasted for hours. They had a lot to catch up on since Ryan hadn't returned home to tell her teacher about how life in the big city was treating her star pupil. She considered Mrs. Dolton a member of her chosen family. The difference between Mrs. Dolton and Sylvie or Viv was that Mrs. Dolton knew who Ryan was before college. Everyone from college only knew what Ryan was comfortable sharing. With Mrs. Dolton, Ryan felt that she could share anything and everything without judgment. If it weren't for her, Ryan was unsure of what her life would be like now.

When Ryan finished her call, she walked out of her room to find Viv in the studio, headphones on, painting frenetically. She approached quietly, leaning against the large doorway that defined the space. It wasn't the first time she'd seen Viv do this. Even still, she was always captivated by the sight.

Viv was always concerned about being as good an artist as Geraldine. She constantly felt inferior; her medium of choice was acrylic paint, rather than oil, which was her mother's preferred choice. On top of that fact, she couldn't shake the feeling that she had to define her point of view uniquely to her persona. As a result, the work she shared with the world was always technically flawless.

When Viv was like this, she wasn't thinking; she wasn't worried. She was feeling. Emoting. Creating. Having the time of her life. Her arms flowing like those of a ballet dancer, head bobbing to the beat, she would dance for a few notes and then stand intensely still, focusing on one section or another.

Just then, Viv danced and spun around to see Ryan staring at her. "Oh, you're done with your call?" she asked, pulling off her headphones and panting from her movements.

"Yep. Just finished."

"Cool. Wanna watch that movie now?" Viv had just bought the Special Collector's Edition DVD of *Footloose*.

Ryan nodded.

"Okay. Gimme a sec to clean myself up a bit. Don't wanna get paint on the couch," Viv said, heading towards the bathroom.

Ryan went to the kitchen and took a deep breath as she opened the fridge. She grabbed two beers, opened them, and took a few big gulps from her bottle before heading back to the couch.

Viv emerged from her room and was ready to hit Play on the remote when Ryan grabbed her hand to stop her.

"Why don't you do that for real?" she asked.

"What? That?" Viv asked, pointing to her canvas.

Ryan nodded.

Viv waved her off. "Because. No one wants to see that shit. Besides, it's just for me. It's like therapy. Cheaper too."

Ryan looked in the direction of the canvases. "I think you're wrong. I think it would be really popular with people. Like a window into the artist's soul." Viv stared back blankly as Ryan continued, "What do you think about when you're in that mode?"

Viv, grabbing the back of her neck, exhaled deeply. "Shit, I don't know, Ry. Anything, everything, nothing. Depends on how I'm feeling. Depends on the song. Different emotions pop up. Frustration, happiness, sometimes sadness. It's just a release of the things I can't find the words for." Viv's brow furrowed as she realized she'd never asked herself these questions before.

"How did you know you were gay?" Ryan blurted out. She shrank slightly into her corner of the couch, embarrassed at how bluntly she had said it and shocked that she had actually asked.

Viv was caught off guard, both by the question and the sudden change of topic. She felt her face get flushed and tried to play it off by clearing her throat. "Ehherrrm, fuck. Throwing hardballs tonight, eh? Um, I don't really know. I just did. In sixth grade, we played spin the bottle at my friend Brandon's birthday party. My spin landed on Mark Thomas. When we kissed, it felt *okay*, I guess, but I didn't understand why everyone made a big deal about kissing. A few rounds later, it was Candice Anderson's turn, and it landed on me. When we kissed, I felt fireworks up and down my skin. I remembered thinking that *THIS* must be what the big deal is about, and I guess I've just been chasing that feeling ever since."

"What about Sylvie?"

Viv tilted her head. "Actually, I don't know. We never talked about it. She was the only other gay person in seventh grade when she moved up from LA, so we were instantly attached at the hip."

Ryan leaned forward slightly. "Did you ever date?"

"Who, Sylvie? Never. Well, sort of, only because people assumed that we were. We kissed once and realized that it was gross. I try to block that part of our friendship out of my head." Viv shook her head at the memory. "Why the interrogation?"

Ryan had run out of follow-up questions. Her eyes dropped to the floor as she sat with her knees to her chest, feet crossed, her beer held with both hands.

Viv sat up straight. "You okay, RyRy?"

Ryan sat solemnly. Unresponsive.

"You can tell me anything. You know that, right?" Viv bent her head, trying to make eye contact.

"What if…" Ryan paused.

"If what?"

"What if I'm gay?" Ryan pursed her lips together immediately after the words left her mouth.

Viv's eyes widened. "Then you'd…just be gay." She threw her hands up in confusion as to why this would be a major revelation for Ryan. A revelation that she'd be scared to say out loud, at that.

"But what do I do? How do I talk to people? I could barely figure out how to date guys properly. And that's the normal thing to do. I mean, I don't even know if I am." Ryan felt herself getting frustrated. "You probably think I'm being stupid." She hung her head down, feeling as though she'd made a fool of herself.

Viv was supportive and reassuring. "Not at all. Everyone has their own journey and story. There's no book that tells you how to come out or be out. We're all figuring it out day by day. Myself included."

Ryan's eyes met Viv's empathetic gaze. "But you do it so well." She paused to choose her next words carefully. "Maybe you could teach me?"

Viv was confused. "Teach you what?"

"How to flirt with women. Who pays on the first date? You know, show me the rainbow ropes."

Is she being serious right now? Maybe I should just tell her how I feel. No, fuck, that's selfish. Fuck my life.

"Rainbow ropes." Viv shook her head, smiling. "Okay. Count me in."

Ryan breathed a deep sigh of relief.

Viv placed her hand on Ryan's knee. "You good?"

"Yeah." Ryan nodded. "I am feeling a little bit like a baby. Is it okay if I lay my head in your lap while we watch the movie?"

"Sure thing, RyRy."

Ryan grabbed the blanket from her end of the couch and draped it over herself and Viv's arm as she laid her head in Viv's lap. "Thanks, Vivi."

Why did I agree to this? Who agrees to coach their crush on how to date other people? Fuck, maybe it won't be that bad.

***

For the next two months, Viv reluctantly played Ryan's Yoda. When they went out, if they weren't at a college party, they'd hit up Henrietta Hudson or Cubbyhole, and Viv would walk Ryan through her thought process when she liked someone.

The particular things that stood out, as compared to the other women. She'd press Ryan to try to do the same in the hopes of finding out if she had a particular type. And, selfishly, to see if she fit that mold or not.

When Ryan did find someone who, in her words, "seemed interesting," Viv encouraged her to ask the person to dance. Ryan always took that direction nervously, but she was never rejected.

Of course they said yes. They always do. Who'd say no to a girl as beautiful as her?

Viv would quietly stew, leaning against the bar while she watched with envy as her pupil was grinding upon the woman du jour. She'd try to not look so obvious, opting to stare at the surroundings or colorful plethora of large paper umbrellas, streamers, bulbs, and other trinkets hanging from the ceiling at Cubbyhole. At times, she'd try flirting with someone, but her eyes would always look past them at Ryan, her hips swaying rhythmically side to side and her dance partner's hands holding on gently to her waist.

Every now and then, Ryan's partners would trace their hands up the tattoo on Ryan's left leg or the serpent that ran across her stomach, connecting her black-and-gray leg sleeve to her colorful arm sleeve. Ryan would always be sexily coy, holding her long, wavy hair back with one hand and smiling shyly. At the end of the song, Ryan would stand up straight, like a soldier, wave to her dance partner, and run hastily back to Viv.

Viv, looking confused, would inevitably ask, "What happened this time?"

"Right!" Ryan would then smack herself in the forehead. "I don't have to wait for *her* to ask me for my number. I can do that too. This looks a lot easier when you and Sylvie do it."

Viv put her head in her hands, amused yet relieved. It was time for a new strategy. The next few nights, Ryan pointed out the woman du jour to Viv, and Viv went over as the wingwoman, explained that her friend was very shy but wanted to ask her out on a date. Viv went on to say that the woman du jour was welcome to write her number on a piece of paper; if she liked dancing with Ryan, then she could hand her the piece of paper. If not, no harm, no foul.

This strategy saw a one hundred percent success rate. While this relieved Viv from personally watching Ryan dance with someone else—she always went outside for a smoke after delivering her lines—she had a new problem. What would she do for the hours that Ryan was on these dates?

What kind of place is she going to take her? What if she's a jerk? What if it goes well? I'm gonna have to be nice to this person.

Viv filled the time painting, reading, smoking on the fire escape, doing homework when school started, or watching TV. The fact that she could've gone on her own dates eluded her. She wanted desperately to tell Ryan how she felt, but believed that that window had closed.

Each date night, Ryan came home and clued Viv in, telling her what they did, what she learned about the person, if they kissed or not, if she wanted to see them again, etc. Viv begrudgingly listened, offering impartial thoughts and advice on what to do next. Typically, Ryan wasn't interested in anyone beyond one or two dates, even though on paper they all seemed great...until she began to see Michaela, a girl who went to Columbia.

Michaela was from Atlanta and was an urban-planning major. She was five foot seven and had long braids she kept in a bun and cocoa-brown skin. She wowed Ryan on their first date with her knowledge of how the grid system came to be in New York, how they ripped up the streets to lay the original subway tracks, and other fun facts about the city, including that the different color grouping of the train lines was an homage to the fact that each group was once a private railroad company before they all went bankrupt and the MTA took over.

Each night, Ryan shared all of the fun facts with Viv. They'd gone on four or five dates, and Ryan seemed pretty smitten, until she came home upset one night.

Viv noticed the look on Ryan's face right away and closed the book she was reading on the couch. "What's wrong?"

"I don't think I'll be seeing Michaela anymore?" Ryan sighed and sat next to Viv.

"Why not?"

Ryan's eyes lowered to the floor. "She dumped me because she said she has no interest in being the first girl I sleep with. We went to her place after dinner, and she tried to initiate sex. Everything was fine...and then...I just freaked out. I don't know why. I can't really explain it. I can't explain it now, and I couldn't in the moment either. I guess she got fed up."

"Geez, I'm sorry she said that. Also, that feels a bit dumb on her part."

Ryan, dewy-eyed, looked up at Viv. "Have you been someone's first girl?"

Viv threw her hands in the air. "Well, yeah! We're nineteen, not forty-eight. There's no way every person you meet has tons of experience at our age. There have been times when I've taken a girl home, and she changed her mind, and we did nothing but cuddle. It was fine. Besides, it's not like it's the only qualifier. You still have to learn your partner's body. What they like, what they don't like. Who cares if you've slept with all of these people if you suck at sex? That's even more embarrassing. Not that *you* have anything to be embarrassed about."

"I know. You're right. I just don't know what to do." Ryan twiddled her thumbs. "She said she's been with four people: one guy, three girls. How many girls have you been with?"

"Twelve." Viv pulled her lips together tightly. *Shit. That came out way too fast.*

"See!" Ryan exclaimed. "That's a ton of expectations to live up to. How am I supposed to compete with numbers like that?"

"It's not about competing against anyone." Viv tried to reassure Ryan by rubbing Ryan's right knee with her hand. "Those other people aren't around for a reason. You don't have to worry about being the same, better, or different than whoever someone slept with before you. You just have to be yourself. Use your instincts."

In what felt like a split second, Ryan moved from her position on the couch and straddled Viv, resting her hands on Viv's shoulders.

Viv cleared her throat. "What, uh…what are you doing?"

"Using my instincts," Ryan said bravely, "and now I don't know what to do next."

"Um, maybe trying with your words this time might be easier?" Viv replied, softly covering the backs of Ryan's hands with her own as her clit and heart throbbed at the same breakneck pace.

"Vivi, I...like you. A lot. I have for a while now. Before, I thought maybe it was just as a friend or a phase, but then I kept having these thoughts about you last year during finals, and I didn't know what to do with them. I didn't grow up with people that openly talked about their sexuality or sexual desires like you do. So I thought, instead of telling you and embarrassing myself, that maybe you could teach me how to be better at being gay so that you'd think I was good enough. Or maybe I'd realize that I didn't like you as more than a friend, and then I could date other girls. Or that I'm just straight. But when you'd take me out and set me up with all those other girls, all I thought about was you. Like tonight, when I was with Michaela, it was fine, but I wanted it to be you, and then I freaked out and stopped it. I really wish I'd chosen a less embarrassing way to tell you all of this than mounting you like s—"

Viv lowered her eyelids and gently moved her hands to gently hold Ryan's face. "I fell for you the moment you stole my drink."

A small smile crept across Ryan's face as Viv moved to kiss her. Viv paused for a half a second as their lips grazed each other's before leaning in for a full kiss. Every fiber in Ryan's body felt as if it were on fire. She'd dreamed about this moment for months, and it was finally happening. Her arms relaxed around Viv's neck, and she slid farther down onto Viv's lap, their bodies pressing against each other. Their heart rates rising as the heat between them grew. Ryan dragged her lips across Viv's cheek as Viv threw her head back. Viv placed several kisses on Ryan's neck while her fingertips rested just underneath the bottom of her shirt.

Ryan leaned backwards and pulled her shirt over her head before saying, "Can you take me to your room?"

"Are you sure? We don't have to. I'm okay waiting."

Ryan nodded. She was nervous, but she was ready.

Viv lifted Ryan off the couch and carried her into her room. She not so gracefully laid her on the bed as she tripped over her unfolded laundry, causing them to bump heads. They shared a laugh at Viv's uncoordinated expense. Viv planted another kiss on Ryan's lips before giving her a reassuring look as she removed her own shirt and sweatpants before carefully removing the rest of Ryan's clothing.

On Viv's Hot Pocket nights, her actions were hasty, quick to get to the action. Not tonight. She paused to take in the full vision. She traced her fingers up Ryan's arm, down across her body, ending at the bottom of her left leg. Ryan held her arms over her head, with her fingers slightly intertwined, and moved side to side with Viv's motions. The streetlights shone through the windows onto the bed and cast a shadow of the window frames across Ryan's body. The sounds of a Saturday night in New York City were in full effect with cars honking, sirens, and the shouting of drunk people. Inside the walls of Viv's room, they heard nothing but the sound of each other's breathing.

Ryan stared back at Viv in wonderment. She could see the wetness drip down Viv's leg and reached for Viv's arm, pulling her closer. Their tongues explored each other's as their breaths became more haggard, more desperate. Viv moved herself farther down the bed, leaving a trail of kisses from Ryan's neck, down her chest, before stopping to flick Ryan's nipple. Ryan let out a soft moan in response to Viv's warm tongue probing her skin. Her body writhed up and down as her desire grew. Viv continued her journey south, licking and sucking her way down past Ryan's belly button. Ryan abruptly stopped her.

Viv looked up, concerned. "Too much? We can stop."

Ryan shook her head. "No. I don't want to stop, but, um, do you think that maybe I could do you first? I know you said it's not a competition, but I think it's better for me this way. It feels like there would be less pressure."

"Yeah. Yeah, of course." Viv raised her eyebrows in amazement. "Do you want to switch?"

Ryan shook her head. "Nope. I want you here," she said, pointing at her mouth.

"Wait…what exactly?" Viv was confused.

"I want you to sit on my face. You haven't done that before?" Ryan asked.

"Not once."

Ryan smiled. "Even better. No expectations."

Viv was the nervous one now. "Okay, what exactly am I supposed to do?"

Ryan motioned with her hand. "Come towards me. Now, place your knees on either side of my head, and drop your butt down a little."

Viv obliged. "Like thiii—"

As she lowered her body down, she felt Ryan's tongue lightly lick her outer lips, before Ryan grabbed Viv's ass with both hands, and her tongue returned with much more forceful strokes from the bottom of Viv's vagina to her clit and back down again. Viv leaned forward and pressed her hands against the wall as she moaned in ecstasy at the sensations coursing through her while Ryan licked, kissed, and sucked every part of her body that was accessible. When she managed to open her eyes, through the hair that hung down around her face she could see Ryan's face buried in her pussy, eyes closed and attention focused.

Ryan briefly opened her eyes, looked up, and locked eyes with Viv, sending fresh lightning rods running through Viv's body. Viv let out a loud gasp when Ryan suddenly inserted her stiff tongue inside of her and grabbed her ass tighter to ride her face. Viv had had a lot of different sexual encounters, but she'd never been tongue fucked before. Her breaths came quicker as Ryan went deeper, each thrust hitting new nerve endings.

A wave of pleasure that Viv had never experienced before washed over her, and her body shook violently as she lost control and came. Viv's body convulsed while Ryan licked up the mess she'd made before she moved Viv's body farther down the bed to lie on top of her. Viv's body melted into Ryan's as she pressed her face to Ryan's neck, still trying to catch her breath.

"Are you sure that was your first time?" Viv asked between gasps.

"Mm-hmm. I did watch a lot of lesbian GIFs on Tumblr though."

Viv laughed hysterically and kissed Ryan deeply while trying to regain her own energy so she could give Ryan the same blissful pleasure.

Holy shit, that was amazing. I knew I felt the spark. Eat shit, Sylvie! Ryan is my penguin love. I can't wait to be happy with her forever.

Chapter 9

Massages

Viv's sophomore and junior years were the happiest of her life. Her love with Ryan blossomed with each passing day. Even though they'd been best friends for months, and despite the fact they already lived together, Viv believed in still having a proper courtship. They had candlelit dinners, walked along the Hudson River, and skated in the park. Anyone who saw them could tell how completely over the moon they were with each other. They converted the second bedroom into Ryan's studio to give each other more space to create.

The love they shared seemed to kick their artistic sides into high gear. Viv began to build a small cult following within the artist community in Chelsea, creating vivid depictions of landscapes from their dates that were burned into her memory. She'd spend the evenings at small galleries, explaining with deep passion and controlled excitement about the magnificent nature of our everyday surroundings, which we take for granted, and the beauty all around us if we get out of our heads and open our eyes.

Meanwhile, Ryan's star reached new heights. She won a design competition their sophomore year; it gave her a slot in New York's Fashion Week, which was to take place during the fall of their junior year, and a small grant to launch her own brand. Viv still remembered the shriek Ryan let out when she opened the email with the news. They splurged and went to Morimoto's to celebrate with Sylvie, who jokingly asked Viv how she felt knowing she'd be Ryan's assistant in a few years. Viv laughed her off. It was no secret that Ryan's star was bigger and brighter than hers. They openly talked about it often. Viv didn't care. Being a supportive partner was an important trait that she learned from her parents. It wasn't a competition, by any means, and she genuinely enjoyed watching Ryan's joy grow as her dreams came closer to reality.

At the end of their sophomore year, Ryan spent the summer in San Francisco and got to see the Roches' mythical love. Geraldine and Henri, having heard stories nonstop on Skype calls with Viv, adored her and welcomed her with open arms. At the airport, she stood back as they greeted Viv and was surprised when they both rushed over in her direction to give her a dual embrace. Ryan, having never lived in an accepting family environment, immediately fell in love with them.

Once in the car, Henri played Al Green's "Let's Stay Together." Viv laughed at the decision before asking, "What did you guys fight about?"

Geraldine laughed as well and said, "Nothing at all, sweetheart. We're just happy you're home."

Viv sang along with her parents for a few moments before her father turned the music down slightly to let Ryan in on the joke. He explained that while he and Geraldine never truly fought, they did have their fair share of disagreements. When one of them decided that they wanted to put the situation behind them, they each played a specific song on their record player. Geraldine's choice was Marvin Gaye and Tammi Terrell's "Ain't No Mountain High Enough," while Henri's was the Temptations' "Ain't Too Proud to Beg." When the other half came to the same conclusion, whether it was an hour later or the next day, "Let's Stay Together" could be heard throughout the apartment. They'd dance in the living room, smiling like teenagers, and then, without the same fiery emotions, they'd eventually revisit the subject that caused the disagreement.

Not only was it easy to see where Viv had learned to communicate with music, but it was the most adorable conflict-resolution strategy that Ryan had ever heard. It was clear they saw each other as equal pieces that made up a full unit. A unit that was now making space for her.

With Ryan's addition, their game nights became more competitive than ever. New rules had to be put in place just so the Roches had a chance of winning against the ringer Viv had brought into the fold. They took Ryan on tours of the city, doing all of the obligatory tourist activities: riding a cable car, walking along Fisherman's Wharf, visiting Alcatraz, and crossing the Golden Gate Bridge. They were also sure to show her the *real* San Francisco, the city that the locals experienced while eating a sub from Vikings in Lakeview, burritos from El Faro in the Mission District, and freezing their butts off at Ocean Beach after having dinner at the Cliff House.

Ryan loved it all. The things she marveled at the most? The sheer beauty of the Palace of Fine Arts, a segment called "Sassy Sports" on 99.7 NOW's morning show, *Fernando and Greg*, and the distinct neighborhoods for Asian culture—most notably, Japantown.

Growing up with Jack didn't allow room for Ryan to get in touch with her mother's heritage. While New York had Japanese restaurants and influence scattered across the city, there was no true Japantown. When she laid eyes on San Francisco's Japantown—an area of only four city blocks, not nearly as expansive as Chinatown—Ryan felt a piece of herself awaken inside. She spent countless days exploring every nook and cranny, spending hours in stores, chatting with locals, learning a few words in Japanese, and trying all the food. Her experiences fed her soul and inspired her to design pieces that were a fusion of Japanese and American women's styles for Fashion Week, to act as the debut of the Ryan Pearce Collection.

Without question, her debut was a smashing success. Viv made space in her studio for Ryan to get an early start on her collection. It worked to Ryan's benefit as she was able to study her reference material and return to the studio to work on it that afternoon. She designed everything from leisurewear that combined elements of a kimono and a woman's suit, to layered dresses inspired by the five-tiered Peace Pagoda that defined Japantown.

Before heading back to New York, Viv asked her dad to help get a proper website up for the show. At the time, Ryan thought it premature, but by the end of the week, her in-box was overflowing with inquiries. She beamed with excitement at how much her work resonated with people. It was one thing for Mrs. Dolton and her professors to praise her work. It was a completely different thing altogether for a city like New York to give her a unanimous stamp of approval.

As much as she enjoyed the success and interest, Ryan wanted to focus on school and not be overwhelmed. She calculated how long it would take for her to make each design and decided that she'd make each piece a limited-edition item. There were only going to be ten pieces made for each of the ten designs. She released ninety for purchase and auctioned the final ten. Ryan's strategy was unbelievably successful. Her business acumen was almost as impressive as her design sensibilities.

Despite early wins, she remained incredibly humble and in lockstep with Viv, who was always there. She lugged rolls of fabric up the stairs when Ryan needed a break from her studio at school, she functioned as not only Ryan's second pair of hands, but also her third and fourth pairs at times as well, and she held Ryan on nights she couldn't sleep because of the stress. In turn, Ryan never let their relationship falter because of her schedule. Date nights were always prioritized, and she never missed one of Viv's openings or forgot to pick out and style Viv's outfit the night before a show because she knew how much a small process like that kicked Viv's anxiety into motion.

Between her internships, school, and spending the summer in San Francisco, Ryan hadn't returned to White Plains since she first moved to the city, and she intended to keep it that way. She and Viv discussed staying in New York for a few years after graduation and building their careers before moving to San Francisco and starting a family.

Ryan's great escape from White Plains was interrupted the summer before their senior year when she was asked to give a speech to introduce her father; he was being honored with an award for decades of mentoring young cadets and molding them into men fit to serve their country. The awarding body, unaware of Jack and Ryan's relationship, or lack thereof, created a mutually unenjoyable experience for both of them. They curtly discussed the arrangements with Jack and effectively wrote the speech. Ryan wanted to spend as little time as possible in White Plains.

The only thing Viv dreaded more than being away from her was the idea of Ryan returning to a past she'd worked so hard to shed. "Do you have to go?" Viv whined, holding Ryan in bed the morning before she left, their legs intertwined. Viv made and then served breakfast in bed, stalling Ryan's departure.

Ryan sighed. "Believe me, I don't want to do this, but it's tradition with this group for children to award their parents. I don't want to leave either." Ryan kissed Viv's shoulder and nuzzled her face before they exchanged soft, sleepy kisses. The sun was officially out, its streaks of light warming the room.

"What if I went with you?" Viv suggested.

Ryan shook her head quickly. "You know you can't. For *so* many reasons. Besides, he dismisses me every chance he gets, and you and I both know you wouldn't be able to keep your mouth shut." She lovingly stroked Viv's arm as she spoke. She knew that Viv was fiercely protective by nature.

"You're right about that," Viv replied, wrapping her legs tighter around Ryan's, staring into her eyes. Talking about Jack always made her sad. For Ryan and for herself. She'd never have the type of bond with Jack that Ryan had with her parents. "If you call him right now and tell him you got your tubes tied last year, he might tell you not to come." She was half joking, but there was also a chance it could work, given Jack's extremist views that a woman's role in society was solely to bear children and serve her husband.

Ryan opened her mouth to make a sarcastic comment when a slew of fire trucks flew down Second Avenue, interrupting the conversation.

Viv threw her free hand up into the air, "Jesus fucking Christ! Why is someone always dying in this city?"

Ryan gently pulled Viv's arm back down and planted a quick kiss on Viv's lips. "Two days, Vivi. That's it. Forty-eight hours. Then I'll be back, and we'll fly to see my adopted parents this weekend and have another amazing summer together."

"Promise?" Viv asked with puppy-dog eyes.

"Promise."

***

Forty-eight hours passed. Viv impatiently waited for Ryan to tell her she was on the train back to the city so she could meet her at Grand Central Station. When her phone finally vibrated, her heart fluttered and quickly sank.

Ryan: I can't do this anymore Vivi. We're over.

Viv called Ryan right away. No answer. She tried again. Straight to voice mail. She tried again. Straight to voice mail. She paced back and forth in the apartment, wondering what could've happened. Her breath quickened. She called Sylvie to ask her to try reaching out to Ryan. Same result. She cried out, her voice bouncing off the walls. She slammed her fists against the wall in frustration. The afternoon heat coupled with Viv's anxiety sent her into a full tailspin and made her feel claustrophobic. She panted as sweat dripped down her body. She had to find out what was happening.

She called her friend Dave, borrowed his car, and drove to White Plains. Each red light couldn't change fast enough. For the next hour, Viv could think of nothing but the millions of scenarios running through her head. She raced up Sprain Brook Parkway, bobbing and weaving between cars. They used to love the tree-lined roadway. They'd go upstate when they needed a break from the city. The endless greenery was always a soothing, welcome sight to Viv, but now, soothing was the furthest thing from Viv's mind as she drove.

As she exited the parkway and drove towards East White Plains, her pain was temporarily suspended by aggravation at the sight of Lake Street. The street was full of one- and two-story buildings with mom-and-pop restaurants, cigar shops, and other neighborhood establishments. What was striking was that every building, lamppost, and street sign had American flags hanging off them. Ryan had mentioned that she grew up near Passidomo Veterans Memorial Park, but she hadn't said anything about the nauseating amount of American spirit present.

When Viv arrived at the Pearce residence on Gainsborg Avenue, she parked haphazardly across the street and jumped out. It was a sleepy street of faded pastel-colored homes with wood siding and sloping roofs, each with a different-colored roof shingle. Most homes displayed their own large American flags from the porch or second floor, while others opted for small flags on their lawns. Ryan's house was stark white and had a proper flagpole off to the right. Viv's heart rate continued to rise as she approached. She grabbed the black wrought-iron railing to steady herself as she climbed the four small steps to ring the doorbell.

She rang it three times and tapped her foot while she waited, arms crossed. She turned as the door opened, to see Jack emerge with his broad shoulders and large frame. Towering over Viv, he stared at her, through the storm door, with his signature scowl. He was more of an intimidating force than she'd imagined. His hair had started to gray and was a tousled mess, as if he'd just woken up. Viv reached to open the storm door. Jack responded by grabbing the handle on the other side, pulling it tight.

Viv spoke up to account for the barrier he was keeping between them. "Hi! Is Ryan here?"

"No," Jack replied flatly. "Who are you?" Even his slightly elevated speaking voice sounded like a roar. It took Viv by surprise.

"My name is Viv…Vivienne. I'm her roommate."

Jack furrowed his brow, unimpressed. "Never heard of you."

Viv pressed on, leaning her hand on the doorframe, "Do you know when she'll be back? I really need to talk to her."

"I don't. Now get the fuck off my property before I call the cops," Jack said as he slammed the door in Viv's face.

Viv gasped in astonishment and sadness. She hung her head and slowly returned to the car. She drove around the corner and cried for what felt like hours, pounding her hands against the steering wheel, before returning to the city.

She returned Dave's keys to him without uttering a word. When he asked if she was okay, she looked briefly at him, teary-eyed, before walking down the stairs of his apartment building. Through pure muscle memory, she walked back to the Bedford Park Station and caught the 4 Line back to Manhattan. She could barely feel the cool plastic against her skin as she took a seat in the center of the car. She stared listlessly out of the opposite window at the endless array of brick apartment buildings in the Bronx, each one barely distinguishable from the next. The flow of people entering and leaving the train at each stop, sitting next to her or across from her, didn't faze her. She kept the same broken look on her face. Those who sat across from her looked away, uncomfortable with the zombie girl staring at them.

The green and blue tiles at her stop, Astor Place, came and went as she was disconnected from her body. She rode the full forty-four stops through Manhattan and to the end of the line at the Crown Heights-Utica Station in Brooklyn. Her trance was only broken by another passenger's tapping her on the shoulder.

"Hey? Ma? End of the line. You gotta get off."

Viv looked into the brown eyes of the kind stranger and stood up in a hurry, brushing past him. Outside of the station, she got her bearings before returning to her trance as she walked for over an hour and a half to cross the Brooklyn Bridge. The endless people she passed by on the street were irrelevant. Her feet began to ache once she crossed back into Manhattan.

After another half hour of walking, she dragged her feet up the stairs and back into her apartment. Once inside, she slid down the door, onto the floor, and resumed sobbing. She couldn't make sense of what was happening around her. The only thing that did make sense was that she couldn't spend the night alone. She changed her flight to leave for San Francisco that night.

***

"I don't understand what went wrong," she cried into her mom's lap on the couch.

Geraldine tried to soothe her heartbroken daughter by rubbing her side. "Oh, I don't know, baby. She seemed like a real sweet girl. Sometimes things happen that we don't understand."

"But we're perfect for each other. What could've happened," Viv exclaimed, her hand smacking the empty cushion just beyond her head.

Henri, squatting in front of the couch, shared an empathetic look with Geraldine and placed his hands on his daughter's. "Ah, sweetheart, I know you thought you'd be together forever. Your mom and I got lucky meeting each other so young. That's more of the exception than the rule. Most people have multiple loves until they find 'the one.' I guess we should've prepared you better for the realities of heartbreak."

They spent the remainder of the evening consoling a sobbing Viv until she finally fell asleep. They'd continue to do so for the ensuing days and weeks. Viv wasn't in the gallery, she wasn't in the studio painting, she didn't want to see Sylvie, and she was barely engaged in their game nights. She spent most of her time holed up in her room, staring at the ceiling. Her heart had collapsed, and her zest for life seemed to vanish with it.

She somberly returned to New York at the end of the summer to find every trace of Ryan gone. All her clothes, the mannequins, her books, and her mugs were nowhere to be found. When school started, Viv hoped to see Ryan and at least get an explanation in person. She spotted Ryan walking off campus in her direction and called out for her. She wore a black headband and black dress. Ryan walked directly past Viv without so much as looking her way or changing her facial expression. Viv turned to watch her continue on to embrace a basic-looking white guy she'd never seen before. Viv's heart broke all over again as she watched him kiss her and wrap his arm around her before they walked away.

Through some sleuthing by Sylvie, she found this Ryan-stealing guy's name was Todd Delisle. He was an NYU MBA student who was also from White Plains. Word on the street was they'd grown up together and reconnected over the summer. None of this made sense to Viv.

Instead of trying to figure it out, Viv decided that she needed a distraction. Every night was a working night, a party night, or both. "Sex, booze, and rock and roll" was her new mantra. Nothing else mattered. Why should it? She'd spent her whole life believing in love, only to have it snatched away in the blink of an eye. On the other hand, her work, alcohol, and a warm body never let her down. They were always there and always understood her and her needs. The inclusion of her work in her new mantra was the sole reason that Viv produced the grades required to graduate, despite her party-animal, hair-of-the-dog lifestyle.

Sylvie, who had broken up with Jen that same summer, did her best to make sure Viv got home safely on the nights that she could. With graduation approaching, Sylvie said the most loving thing she'd said up to that point in their lives, "Viv, I love you. You're my best friend on this stupid Earth. I can tell that this version of you and this lifestyle aren't going to stop anytime soon. I'm not judging you, but I'm moving back home. I can't watch you end up in a gutter somewhere if I'm not here."

Viv looked at her friend with tear-filled eyes.

Sylvie continued, "So you're coming back with me. I already found a two-bedroom for us. A big one. Nonnegotiable."

Viv nodded and leaned her head on Sylvie's shoulder. It was officially time to put her hopeless romantic dreams to bed.

At their commencement ceremony, when Viv saw Ryan in passing amidst the sea of red caps and gowns, she was convinced that would be the last time they'd ever see each other.

Chapter 10
I Hated That Dress

Viv's eyes shot open. "Gabby…what the fu…" Viv's voice trailed off as she watched Ryan nervously enter the roll-up doors to the studio.

"It's gonna be fine. Trust me," Gabby replied, tapping Viv quickly on the knee. "Dylan, go greet Ryan, and bring her over to us, please."

Dylan was Gabby's assistant. He was a wiry, blond, curly-haired, catty, little twink who irked Viv to no end. He worked his ass off though—there was no denying that—which made him invaluable to Gabby. Given how much he loved to gossip, it was only because of Gabby's obsession with NDAs that Viv's business didn't end up on the streets.

"Do you need a morning go-go, Boss?" Zo asked. Viv's morning go-go was orange juice and tequila with a splash of champagne.

"Yes, please," Viv said as she sighed and leaned back against the couch.

Her nightmare had come to life. As Ryan approached, Viv's heart sank to her stomach, and she felt herself becoming more and more anxious. Ryan looked barely older than she did in their college days. She wore an oversized red jacket, black ripped jeans, and black Converses, her hair swept to one side. Viv hunched over and pressed her thumbs against her forehead.

Gabby rose to greet her. "Ryan, I'm Gabby. We spoke on the phone." She stretched out her hand and gave Ryan a hearty handshake. "So glad you could make it on short notice. Here. You can have my seat." She gestured to her spot next to Viv and moved to pull up an ottoman to sit in front of them.

"Hi, Vivi," Ryan said softly.

Viv sat in silence, refusing to make eye contact. Teeth clenched.

Gabby broke the silence, "You made quite an entrance last night."

"Here you are, Boss," Zo said, returning with her drink.

"Thank you, Zo," she replied, wasting no time by taking a large gulp before transitioning to sipping the drink. She stared at her glass as she spoke, "Why are you here? You know what? I don't care. Gabby, why did you bring her here?"

"Viv, listen. This isn't a bad thing. It doesn't matter why she came. What matters is what we can do now that she is here. I know you don't think you went anywhere, but this show *was* your comeback. The entire team is fielding calls on when people can schedule your next show. We're at fever pitch. I'm talking four to six months out, at this point, if we say yes to everything. The show was the showstopper you wanted, and Ryan's disruption was the cherry on top. Artistic theater that people crave. They can't get enough of this mystery woman, and we need to capitalize on it all." Gabby spoke with excitement, a glimmer in her eye.

It was hard to discern whether the excitement was for Viv or for her cut of the upcoming shows. Viv didn't care one way or another. "Can you stop speaking in tongues and tell me what you're actually talking about?" Viv looked up at Gabby with her piercing eyes, signaling that whatever patience she walked in with was now gone.

"We're gonna sell you two as an item." Gabby grinned, nodding with her eyebrows raised.

"ABSOLUTELY not," Viv protested.

"Absolutely YES," Gabby countered.

Viv squinted her eyes and leaned in Gabby's direction. "Why would you think I'd agree to this? Convince me."

"Viv"—Gabby sighed before emphatically continuing—"your career was in the shitter two years ago. You know it. I know it. The entire art world and your fans know it. We've been struggling to get you back where you belong. On top! You've done these bullshit, kitschy-themed shows that were crowd pleasers, but had no point of view. No real emotion. No *Viv*. This show was our first step back to peak Viv. With your reputation…a love interest can accelerate things even faster. People love a love story. Hate it all you want. You know I'm right."

Viv knew everything Gabby said was true, but still hated the idea. She hated publicity stunts. She'd rather have her fame based on artistic merits. "We can't find a look-alike and do the same thing?"

"We don't have time for that," Gabby said, shaking her head.

"So I'm whoring myself out for fame now? Zo, another go-go, please," Viv said, handing her empty glass in his direction.

"On it," he said, grabbing the glass and scurrying away.

"You whore yourself out on your own just fine for less," Gabby quipped. "This is just your heart."

Viv put her head back in her hands before addressing Ryan, still refusing to make eye contact. "How much is she paying you to do this? Whatever it is, I'll double it to make you go away."

"Noth-nothing at all," Ryan said, clearing her throat.

"So what's in it for you?" Viv asked.

"What do you mean, what's in it for her?" Dylan interrupted. "She gets to be attached to one of the biggest artists in the world right now. That alone is enough to boost her profile. Plus, it'll make people care about whatever basic, fledgling fashion proj—"

"HEY!" Viv sat up straight, pointing with her arm fully extended in Dylan's direction. "If she's working on something, there's no fucking way it's basic or fledging, no matter how small it is. Someone get this kid away from me. Thank you, Zo."

Zo had returned with a second morning go-go; he ushered Dylan away.

Viv sipped on her drink in between deep breaths as she tried to calm herself. Her outburst had led to a tense silence. She knew she was beat. Damned if you do, damned if you don't. "How long do I have to do this publicity stunt?"

"Not long. A few weeks. Months maybe," Gabby said nonchalantly. "We just need to ride the wave while we have it."

Viv shook her head, trying to make peace with it in her mind. "I can still sleep with whoever I want if I agree to this bullshit, right?"

Gabby knew she'd won now. "Yes, of course. We'll have to be more discreet than usual to make this look legitimate. That goes for the both of you. Understand?"

Viv nodded.

Ryan followed suit.

"And no PDA or I'm out. This is business," Viv added.

"Done," Gabby replied. "Now that we're in agreement, I need you to go shower off the smell of whoever you slept with and switch into the clothes I left for you in your changing room. You two have an interview to get to."

"With who?"

"Susana. You owe her one."

***

Viv, Ryan, and Gabby stepped off the elevator into Susana's office. Her office was a combination of pristine white walls, light-gray carpeting, glass tables and desks, and bright, colorful chairs.

"Viv! Long time no see," the receptionist, Kiara, said with lustful eyes upon seeing her. They'd fucked in the supply closet five years ago during the office holiday party. She was too clingy for Viv, who, after that, requested that all interviews with Susana happen at her studio or a neutral location.

"Hey. Yeah, good to see you too," Viv said quickly, trying to stay focused on the task at hand.

Susana appeared from her office and smiled from ear to ear while greeting them. "Look at the two of you! Smitten as ever. You're not gonna bite my head off this time are you, Viv?"

Viv cracked a fake smile. "Best behavior. Scout's honor."

"Thanks, Gab," Susana said, winking at Gabby before leading them to an interview room.

Viv and Ryan sat on the fuchsia couch, opposite Susana in her black swivel chair. Gabby sat off to the side, in the corner, and was on her phone. Viv sat with her legs crossed, her ankle resting on her knee, and her arm extended across the top of the couch in Ryan's direction. Ryan sat with her legs extended and ankles crossed, her left hand resting on Viv's knee. They had gone over the mechanics of placement and positioning prior to leaving the studio.

Susana started her recording and conducted the interview, following the questions scribbled on her notepad. Viv and Ryan recounted their relationship—how it started, how they met, the love they shared, their summer in San Francisco together, and Ryan's backstory. Viv steeled herself throughout the interview, letting Ryan talk about the touchy-feely questions, while she handled the practical portions.

Gabby was pleased with the way the interview was going. Viv was playing the part and staying calm, while Ryan shone throughout the interview.

"So"—Susana paused—"Viv, I guess I was wrong. You have been in love before. Your story is so beautiful, and your love seems so pure. What happened between you two?"

Gabby's eyes peered over her phone upon hearing the question, hoping that Viv stayed on script. She knew things could go off the rails very quickly.

Viv's spine stiffened, and the hair on the back of her neck stood up. Ryan removed her hand from Viv's knee and opened her mouth to answer just as Viv interjected, "I cheated. You know me, Susie Q. I got greedy. I got caught, and I lost the most amazing woman in my life. Stupidest decision I've ever made. Simple as that."

"And you haven't seen each other since you graduated?"

Viv shook her head. "Nope. Not once."

"And you're able to forgive and trust her again after all these years?" Susana asked Ryan.

Ryan relaxed her shoulders and placed her hand back on Viv's knee. "You know, things change. People grow; they reflect and gain some perspective. I think the time apart will actually allow us to grow closer now. People do stupid things when they're young. And then we end up carrying that regret subconsciously every day because we're too afraid to put ourselves out there. I think everyone deserves a second chance."

"Beautiful." Susana smiled while stopping the recorder. "Well, I think we've got it."

They stayed in the interview room to take a few photos for the article and to exchange pleasantries until Gabby signaled that it was time to head to their next interview. Once in the elevator, Viv's cheery demeanor disappeared. In the car, they rode in silence side by side in the back seat, Viv staring out the window.

"Why did you lie?" Ryan asked, facing Viv. She knew that Viv was going to answer the question about why they broke up, but Viv had not used the explanation Gabby prepared.

Viv responded in a monotone voice, never moving her eyes away from the window. "About what? Why we broke up or the last time we saw each other?"

"Both."

"Because"—Viv paused to choose her words carefully—"I'm used to being scrutinized by the press. You're not. You don't want them to paint you as the villain. You'll go mad trying to defend yourself."

"Thanks," Ryan said, reaching across to grab Viv's hand softly.

Viv snatched her hand away quickly and glared at Ryan, seeing her fully for the first time. She looked just as beautiful as she did the day they met in the cafe. She had a small scar on the left side of her forehead, and her long, wavy hair was interspersed with streaks of gray. Despite the external resemblance to the woman she once loved, Viv sensed that something was absent internally. Her anger restricted her from having a passing thought to inquire and empathize. Ryan stared back with sorrow in her eyes, and Viv knew they were thinking of the same thing.

"Hurts, doesn't it?" Viv said flatly as she rested her head against the window, letting the vibrations of the road rattle her as they continued to their next destination.

Chapter 11

King of Anything

"Go talk to her," Sylvie said, pushing Viv into the courtyard.

It was a cold February afternoon in White Plains. Viv had kept her distance during the funeral proceedings. She stood behind several military servicemen in uniform and watched the flag-covered casket get placed over the grave. Then she covered her ears during the formal gun salute and listened to the playing of taps. As the military-funeral protocols were completed, she peered curiously at the folding and presentation of the American flag.

The wind whipped against Viv's face as she headed to her car. She'd forgotten how cold the winters were on the East Coast. She felt relief and dread once inside the vehicle. Sylvie had guilted her into coming to the funeral.

I should just go home now. I shouldn't be here.

She drove to the site of the repast. It was a single-story meeting hall with big banquet rooms. She kept to herself in the corner of the main hall, grabbing hors d'oeuvres as they passed by and passively waving to familiar faces. Sylvie finally spotted her and walked with her towards the courtyard.

Through the glass, Viv saw Ryan for the first time in ten years. In a long-sleeved, formfitting, knee-length black dress and short black heels, she was standing alone in the center of the garden.

Ryan had just finished saying goodbye to a large group of guests and had ventured into the courtyard for a quiet moment. She was staring at the ground despondently when she heard footsteps approaching. She turned and saw Viv standing a sizable distance away and looking like a deer in the headlights. Ryan's eyes lit up momentarily before she composed herself. Viv looked just as she remembered, standing motionless in her black jumpsuit and overcoat.

A few additional moments passed before Ryan broke the silence. "You came," she said with slight optimism in her voice.

Viv cleared her throat and grabbed at the back of her neck. "Yeah, um, Sylv said that it was the right thing to do. Jack was a total asshole, from what you told me about him, but he was still your dad. I came to show my respects to you. Not him."

"I really appreciate it." Ryan took a few steps closer as she spoke, "You know, after his heart attack, I spent every day in the hospital with him. I don't know why, really. Maybe it was because it was the most time we'd ever spent together, even if he was sedated and asleep for the majority of it. I still remember the last thing he said to me. It was the day before he died. He grabbed my hand and said, *'You're actually a kid that I could be proud of, if you weren't a girl.'*" Her voice trailed off as she finished her sentence, her eyes lowering to the ground.

Viv's body language shifted as she felt Ryan's sadness and neglect, from her birth up until her father's death. "Oh, Ry," she said, grabbing her hand to comfort her, "I'm so sorry. I can't—"

Staring with wide eyes at Viv, Ryan snatched her hand away quickly and snapped, "What are you doing? Someone might see."

Viv's demeanor immediately shifted from empathetic to offensive. "Are you fucking kidding me right now? Jack's dead. You don't give a shit about these people, and yet you still care what they think. You're pathetic." Her rage grew as she spoke, and she turned to walk back into the main hall.

"I'm divorcing Todd," Ryan blurted out.

Viv laughed and turned to reface Ryan. "No, you're not. You chose this stupid bullshit all-American lifestyle. Why change now?"

"Well, I'm doing it," Ryan responded assertively.

"And I'm supposed to care? All I hear is you unceremoniously leaving someone for no good reason...*again*. Please enlighten me. Why should I give a shit?" Viv placed her hands on her hips in irritation.

"Vivi, I—"

"I really don't care what you have to say," Viv interrupted. "I'm getting married."

Ryan was taken aback by Viv's announcement. She tried to find her words. "N-n-n-no, you're not."

"YES. I am. This New Year's Eve. Get divorced. Don't get divorced. I don't care. Just do it away from me." Viv turned once again to leave the courtyard.

Ryan's pride, hurt by both Viv's dismissal and her announcement, couldn't let Viv have the last word. "You're not the only woman I've been with, you know!"

Viv momentarily stopped pacing. While it was disgusting for her to think that Ryan had been wasting her sex life with the same guy for the past ten years, this new information drove a fresh knife through her heart.

Fuck you, Ryan.

Ryan, with tear-filled eyes, watched Viv disappear back into the main hall and grab a glass of champagne from the waiter who passed by as she entered through the doorway.

"Heeeey, Madison! Long time no see. I was just about to head back into the city…" Viv's voice faded as she moved farther away.

***

"Hi, honey. How was the funeral?" Geraldine asked as she picked Viv up after she returned early from New York.

"Fine," Viv responded curtly.

"How was the flight?"

"Fine," Viv responded, still in a huff.

Geraldine knew that Viv's mood was undoubtedly precipitated by seeing Ryan again. She was only like this when she was angry or heartbroken. In this case, it was both. Although they'd maintained a close relationship throughout the years, discussing her daughter's post-Ryan love life had become analogous to traversing an active battlefield full of land mines. She placed her hand on her daughter's knee and patted it lightly. "You know you don't have to get married so quickly."

"I know I don't *have* to, Mom. I *want* to."

"And you feel Alana is *the one* for you?" Geraldine pressed.

Viv sighed deeply. "She's the best one I've got. She always shows up for me. She understands my needs. My wants. Isn't that what matters?"

"Yes, but remember, love doesn't need excuses. Does she make you happy like—" Geraldine stopped herself from saying Ryan's name since it was clear that their reunion had done more harm than good. It wasn't a secret that she and Henri adored Ryan and Ryan them.

It also wasn't a secret that they had their reservations about Alana. While publicly, they were their usual warm and welcoming selves, privately they wondered about her intentions. She was never rude or cold, but Alana always seemed to have the right answer, the right suggestion or formula. It was as if she had turned Viv into an algorithm, engineered to react just as she wished. Viv's artistic vision began to shift from her own point of view to what Alana thought was best, which was always focused on expanding Viv's reach, rather than on the message of the art itself.

She reveled in being the contrarian, as compared to everyone else in Viv's world. She was the only one who referred to Viv as Vivienne on a regular basis. "Vivienne is the name of a refined artist," she'd quipped once. The first few family dinners they had together, she playfully pronounced Henri's name as *hen-ree*, instead of *awhn-ree*, which irked Geraldine to her wits' end.

Though Geraldine and Henri were both well known in their respective fields during Viv's childhood, their public profiles had grown as well. Geraldine had shifted from full-time artist to tenured professor at Stanford, while Henri had risen through the ranks to become a senior vice president at Intel. His interests had expanded from just his duties at work. Every year, for over a decade, he invested a percentage of his annual bonus in emerging start-ups that looked promising. He had a knack for spotting hidden gems in the Silicon Valley, and seven of the companies he invested in either were acquired or went public. He'd turned four- and five-figure investments into multimillion dollar returns.

Despite their newfound wealth, they desired the simple life they'd always had. They never moved from the apartment they raised Viv in. They wore the same clothes and ate at the same restaurants. With more money than they needed and Viv having a wildly successful career, they set up a foundation to continue supporting the arts and sciences.

While Alana managed her way through family time well enough, she was always willing to "help" with the foundation. She sought to learn as much as she could, all while demonstrating that she could pull her weight in the family business.

Geraldine's desire to protect her daughter never waned, no matter how old Viv grew. But she also knew some battles superseded others. Viv's depression in the summer after her breakup with Ryan still haunted her, and Geraldine saw the warning signs again that day.

Don't press it, Gerry. She's healthy; she's happy. What's meant to be will be.

"If you are happy, honey, that's all I care about," she said softly.

"Lana *does* make me happy, Mom," Viv replied calmly. "I wouldn't have been with her this long if I wasn't one hundred percent sure that I wanted to marry her."

Chapter 12

Magic Hands

Viv didn't get married.

On October 8, 2017, two months before the wedding, Geraldine and Henri Roche were killed in a mass shooting in the North Beach District of San Francisco.

It was your typical day in the city, sixty-two degrees with a light breeze. Geraldine and Henri were on one of their usual weekend lunch dates. It was a tradition they had had for years; they would decide on a new neighborhood each weekend to continuously learn of new hidden gems in their city.

Every so often, Viv would join them for a family date. This weekend, however, between her show debuting in two days and the new canvas technology she'd been obsessing over with Henri, she'd asked for a rain check on lunch until the following weekend.

The restaurant was humming along as usual, glasses clinking and tables being bussed, when havoc broke loose. The shooter was twenty-two-year-old Scott Tanner. He was seeking retaliation for being dumped by his girlfriend, who was a waitress at the restaurant that had been chosen by the Roches for their date.

Henri lunged to protect Geraldine when he heard the gunshots. His efforts weren't enough. He was struck twice in the back, while she was struck once in the neck. They died before the police and paramedics arrived. There were six other fatalities and seventeen casualties; the ex-girlfriend went unscathed. While the madness unfolded and the typical cries for gun control sprang up across the Internet, the media painted the shooter as a mentally-ill kid who otherwise had a good upbringing in an upper-middle-class, White household.

Gabby was the one who answered the phone at the studio when the police called. The hair on the back of her neck stood up, and her heart dropped to her stomach as she heard their words come through the receiver. Her hands shook as she put the phone down. She slowly turned to face Viv, who was in the arena, testing the setup for her show. Gabby leaned over with her hands on her desk. She shook her head from side to side and took several deep breaths before she closed her eyes, slammed the desk with her hand, and hung her head down. She stood up straight to compose herself, grabbed at the ends of her jacket, and walked slowly into the arena.

Gabby stared teary-eyed at Viv, who had been so excited about the upcoming show when she'd come into the studio that day. She'd made a few minor tweaks after thinking about the setup overnight and wanted to do some test runs to try it out before making a final decision. Gabby watched the practice run for a few moments before she motioned to the crew to cut the test short.

Viv, flailing in the air, whipped her head around in confusion before finding Gabby at the edge of the arena floor. She still landed on the ground in high spirits from the run-through, but had no clue why Gabby interrupted the rehearsal. She'd never done that before. She knew business matters were off-limits until they were done. "What's up, Gab?" she asked, walking over in Gabby's direction, panting to catch her breath.

"Viv, I think you should sit down," Gabby softly replied.

Time stopped completely. Viv sat stoically in shock before denying the truth of what Gabby was saying. She stood up from the couch, waving off the news, but Gabby pulled at her arm to get her to sit back down. Trying to remain strong for Viv, Gabby showed her on one of their iPads the news coverage of the shooting. As they watched, the names of the victims streamed across the ticker at the bottom of the screen. Third and fourth on the list read "Henri Roche" and "Geraldine Roche." Viv broke down upon the sight of their names.

All activity in the studio stopped in a split second. A cold silence blanketed the space. As Viv collapsed into Gabby's arms with tears streaming down her face, the rest of the studio looked on in shock and sadness. They stood solemnly, keeping a significant distance away from their boss and friend, tears in their eyes, and consoling each other. Viv treated them like family. Viv's success was their success. And her devastation, theirs.

Viv's world faded from color into black-and-white. Her parents had been her entire world. Every step of the way, no matter the circumstance. They were collectively her rock. Her center. Her anchors. Losing one parent would've been akin to losing a limb for her, but to lose both? She hadn't ever been able to fathom a day when they'd no longer be around. In her eyes, they had decades left. There was so much more for them to do and see. So many ways that Viv wanted to make them proud. Her mind began to spiral. No more game nights. No late-night texts and inside jokes. No family dinners. No walking her down the aisle. No playing with their grandkids.

Alana arrived at the studio shortly after the news broke and tried to comfort Viv with Gabby before taking her home. Zo carried her to the car after she said she couldn't feel her legs. That night, Viv cried in Alana's arms for hours in her apartment. Alana soothed Viv the best she could, rocked her in her arms, and softly stroked her hair. She only moved after she insisted Viv eat something.

Upon returning with tomato bisque, Viv's favorite, she tried to get her to eat while talking about more practical matters. "Baby," Alana said softly, "I know you're upset, but we need to call your parents' lawyers to make sure everything is set up right."

Viv's eyes, delirious from grief and lack of food, darted in Alana's direction, and she replied flatly, "Why wouldn't it be? I'm an only child."

That fact didn't seem to matter to Alana. "Yes, but have you seen it with your own eyes?"

"Yes." Viv had no interest in the conversation, nor the energy to have it, but she knew that her reply was correct. Geraldine lost their second child after she was diagnosed with stage 2 ovarian cancer when Viv was a toddler. With their mortality at the forefront of his mind, Henri had a trust set up during her mother's chemotherapy, and they updated it religiously every year. Viv was too young to remember how the chemo affected her mom, but since she'd turned twelve, they had both been adamant that she be involved in their annual review of the trust. The answer didn't seem to suffice for Alana, who pressed on still.

"Okay. Okay, that's good," Alana responded while nodding calculatingly. "Then we should transfer their assets into our names ASAP."

Viv, taking small sips of her soup, still wasn't following. "Lana, we don't have joint accounts yet, remember?"

Alana waved her off. "Yes, yes, honey. I know, but not to worry. I already called Geno at the bank this afternoon. I made an appointment in the morning to get everything squared away…"

Alana continued to talk but Viv heard none of it. Staring at Alana, she no longer saw the confident, sexy go-getter. Instead, the woman in front of her was unrecognizable. Someone who was cold, cunning, and manipulative. She saw the person from whom Geraldine had been trying to protect Viv the day she returned from Jack's funeral.

Viv clenched her teeth and stared at her fiancée with the heat of a thousand suns. She furrowed her brow and took deep, pensive breaths. "Get...out," Viv said firmly in a low tone.

Taken aback by Viv's statement, Alana quizzically responded, "Excuse me?"

Viv threw the bowl of soup against the wall, sending ceramic shards and droplets of soup throughout the living room. "My parents are dead, and the only thing you care about is their *fucking* bank accounts? Take your shit! Keep your ring. Leave your key. And. Get. The. Fuck. OUT!" she roared furiously.

Alana, having never seen this level of rage from Viv, jumped backwards, stumbling over the coffee table. "Honey...I—"

"OUT!" Viv yelled louder this time.

As Alana hastily left the apartment, Viv dropped into a squat, sobbing uncontrollably. For the first time in her life, she was completely alone. Even though Viv was known for being the life of the party and for possessing an infinite Rolodex of contacts, there were only a trusted few with whom she shared her deepest thoughts and feelings—her parents, Alana, Gabby, Sylvie, to a certain extent Zo, and previously Ryan. She couldn't stay for a second longer in her condo and couldn't bear the pain she would experience if she went to her parents' apartment. With Sylvie still on a plane back to San Francisco after hearing the news while away on business in New York, Viv headed to the only other place that felt like home—her studio.

She sat in the center of the arena, staring up like a wide-eyed child at the canvases around her. She thought of all the tireless hours she'd spent with Henri while preparing and perfecting everything leading up to the show, the family car rides to her art exhibitions as a child, the flights to New York for every gallery opening when she was in college, the trips to the Botanical Gardens in the spring, and the stories they her told about falling in love. How'd they'd sweetly coo their nicknames, Gerry and Onnie, to one other. How they'd sing "Let's Stay Together" after every disagreement was put to rest.

Viv's mind was racing as she struggled to come to terms with two lives relegated to no more than memories now. She wiped her tears, walked into the fabrication area of her studio, and grabbed a long knife. She held it out at her side as she walked back into the arena. She placed it between her teeth while she strapped herself into her harness, as she'd done a thousand times before, the clicking of the locks echoing in the empty space. She climbed up to one of the ledges she used as a launchpad and took in the view as she removed the knife from her mouth and held it in both hands.

Without much thought, she launched herself off the ledge, arms outstretched in front of her, towards one of the canvases. She felt the initial resistance before hearing the rip of the canvas as the knife made contact and slid down towards the floor, widening the gash. One by one she repeated the process with each canvas until they were all torn and unusable. Viv, panting from her destruction and barely blinking, was a woman possessed by an overflow of emotions. She dropped the knife in the middle of the arena, unhooked herself, and ventured back into the fabrication studio.

She emerged from the rear of the studio, wheeling a cart holding two freshly primed eight-by-eight regular canvases that were intended for a benefit show the following week. She clumsily maneuvered the large canvases onto the floor, side by side. Another trip to the back of the studio was necessary to mix several gallons of black paint. Once complete, she returned to where the canvases lay. She poured the paint into the paint tray and covered long paint rollers in them. Section by section, she applied the paint. The pristine white canvases transformed to jet-black with each stroke of the roller.

Viv was in a trancelike state. Each stroke held another memory that coursed through her veins. Each movement felt as if she were bidding her happiness farewell. The tears continued to flow down her face. She covered each canvas in two coats of paint as the night began to give way to dawn.

Gabby and the staff and crew arrived at the studio in the morning. Not to work, since Gabby had sent them all home until further notice, but simply to be together. To figure out what they could do for Viv. When they rolled the doors up, they were more than surprised to find their leader sitting stoically in her usual black director's chair, just behind the newly painted canvases, her hand resting curiously across her mouth and covered in black paint. She hadn't slept at all.

Gabby stretched her arm out behind her to signal to the rest of the crew to stay back as she approached Viv. "Viv?" she said softly as she grabbed Viv's hand. "What are you doing here? You should rest."

Viv didn't flinch.

Gabby continued, "Don't worry. I'll cancel the show tomorrow. We can just focus on the arrangements for your parents."

Viv's expression didn't change. "Have the crew paint the edges and the backs of the frames," she said motioning to the canvases. "We're not doing that show, but we're not canceling either. Have them tear the arena down and get these up ASAP…" She pointed towards the arena as her voice trailed off.

Gabby's mouth dropped when she followed Viv's hand to see her handiwork from the night before. She knew how much that project meant to her and Henri. She responded tepidly, understanding that her client, whom she was personally entrusted by Geraldine's agent to look after, was close to becoming fully unhinged. "I…if you're sure, Viv, then I'm sure," she stammered. "Are we renaming the show too?"

Viv nodded. *"Geraldine and Henri."* She had nothing more to say as she excused herself for a cigarette, refusing hugs from her crew, who painfully looked on. Their boss, drinking buddy, jokester, sister, and friend had been broken, and there was nothing they, or anyone, could do to ease her pain.

Chapter 13

You Never Liked Parasailing

Geraldine and Henri was more of a tribute and love letter than a show. Viv instructed Gabby to refund the tickets they'd previously sold and reserved the first several rows for their closest family and friends, along with the families of those who were injured or killed in the shooting.

Attendees who had previously seen one of Viv's shows entered and were instantly perplexed. Gone was the typically elaborate setup they'd come to expect. In its place, facing the audience, were two simple black canvases, side by side, with ladders and ledges adjacent to them. Sylvie, who had barely been able to get a word out of Viv after her plane landed, sat front and center, somberly in anticipation, unsure of what to expect from her best friend.

Viv appeared in her typical black leotard and faced the audience. She placed both hands to her mouth and gestured a kiss towards the audience before turning to face the canvases. She took a deep breath as the first track began to play. The soothing sounds of the Temptations' "My Girl" floated through the speakers. It was one of her parents' favorite songs. Viv moved with as much joy as she could muster as photos of her and her parents were projected above her against the far wall of the arena.

She told the love story of her parents as she gracefully emoted streaks of deep blue, orange, and gold across the canvases, some strokes contained on one and others traversing both surfaces. As she painted, she was filled with memories of her parents' dancing around their tiny apartment, of family vacations and of Christmas mornings. She let those feelings guide her through the Supremes' "Can't Hurry Love," Natalie Cole's "This Will Be," Marvin Gaye's "How Sweet It Is," and Percy Sledge's "When a Man Loves a Woman," imitating their dance moves and facial expressions.

When the final track, Whitney Houston's "I Will Always Love You" started to play, Viv's movements slowed considerably. Though her parents enjoyed this song, just as most of the world did, this wouldn't have made their playlist. This was the only way that Viv could express a small fraction of her emotions. She forced the brushes to move slower and more methodically across the canvases. As the song continued, her emotions visibly began to well up inside of her to an uncontrollable level. Her hands became shaky, her motions disjointed. She'd perched herself atop one of the ledges for the iconic note that occurs two-thirds of the way through the song. Then, Viv flung herself off the ledge and created two long orange and gold brushstrokes down both canvases.

When she reached the ground, the brushes fell from her hands. She dropped to her knees and fell forward with her arms stretched over her head, her forehead against the floor. She audibly wailed until the track was long finished.

The audience looked on in sympathetic silence as Viv's body rose and fell with emotion. Sylvie left her seat at the same time that Gabby walked into the arena, both meeting Viv where she lay in the center. They leaned their heads against Viv, comforting her and coaxing her to stand.

Viv managed a few deep breaths to compose herself before standing to face everyone. She motioned quickly and soberly to the crowd, using the same motion with which she'd started the tribute show, before hastily heading backstage with Sylvie's and Gabby's arms around her.

The reception that followed was a far cry from the typical upbeat atmosphere in which Viv was the life of the party. Instead, Viv sat in her usual chair as guests came and expressed their sorrow and best wishes for her. Gabby facilitated the silent auction, as she would have after any show, with one exception. The proceeds would go to cover funeral costs, hospital bills, and provide financial assistance to the affected families. Viv pledged to match the amount raised with her own money.

The winning bidder simultaneously claimed both canvases and the record for the largest amount ever paid for one of Viv's pieces. The bidder, feeling that the pieces should belong to no one but Viv, elected to remain anonymous and gifted the paintings back to her. This generosity encouraged the losing bidders to donate their bids as well to the families of the injured and deceased and to groups advocating for gun control across the state. Viv kept her promise and matched the amount, dollar for dollar—not only the winning bid, but the amounts donated by the other bidders as well.

The funeral, held one week later, was another blur to Viv. The service seemed to last forever. So many people wanted to speak about Geraldine and Henri. How Geraldine gave someone their first job at an art gallery. How Henri was a trusted mentor and friend in the workplace. Childhood memories from their siblings. Viv may have been the center of their world, but their impact was felt far beyond her existence. Geraldine and Henri were universally loved by anyone with whom they'd spent more than five minutes.

Viv gave the eulogy and spoke of just how deep their love for one another and their community ran. She shared private moments and inside jokes between them. As she spoke, she scanned the faces in the room, not just taking note of who was present and who wasn't, but searching for one face in particular. By the time the service, burial, and repast were over, Viv was completely exhausted.

When Sylvie ushered the final guest out, Viv looked at her with wide eyes. Sylvie, knowing what she was thinking, placed a hand on her shoulder and said sadly, "I'm sorry, Viv. She didn't come."

***

The days, weeks, and months that followed were the darkest of Viv's life. She disappeared from the public eye. Unfortunately, the drama with Alana didn't fade as easily. Susana had been covering the lead-up to their impending nuptials, and the end result was supposed to be a breakout piece for her career. She reached out to Gabby for a comment when Alana was noticeably missing from the tribute show and funeral proceedings.

Gabby said, "No comment."

Susana reached out to Alana to ask about what dissolved their relationship.

Alana, ever the opportunist, went on the offensive. She was quoted as saying, "Viv's a petulant, self-absorbed child. How can anyone love that?" After this, Alana's circle coined the term La Roach for Viv.

"How can anyone love that?" It was a phrase that was burned into Viv's mind, but she didn't respond. She didn't care. About Alana. About art. About anything. She became a hermit. She only left the house to buy more alcohol in bulk or to go to Geraldine's and Henri's gravesides. She'd arrive with a lawn chair and perch there for hours, alternating between sitting silently in her hooded windbreaker or hunching over and talking to them late into the night.

More often than not, Gabby or Sylvie would receive a call from the night grounds manager, Nick, to tell them that Viv had fallen asleep there again. They'd take a rideshare to the cemetery to retrieve her and drive Viv and her car home. They had to work as a team since it was the only way to get Viv's limp body off the ground and to combat her resistance to going home. They got in the habit of bringing a blanket to cover her shivering body, wet from the dew and fog that rolled through during the night.

It was only during those retrieval missions that they were sure that Viv was eating. She'd lost twenty pounds over several months. She became unrecognizable to anyone around her. Except to Sylvie, who'd seen this before. Viv had the same catatonic gaze that she had after Ryan broke her heart. Only, this wound was exponentially deeper and, unlike a broken heart, would never heal.

Gabby canceled all of her upcoming shows. Sylvie, knowing how Viv's behavior and outlook on life had changed when she was trying to get over the breakup, patiently comforted Viv as she slowly coaxed her back to painting. From their photo albums, she picked out pictures of Geraldine and Henri with friends and had Viv use them as reference photos. She didn't need to create the chaotically beautiful art that people had come to expect. For Viv, this was back to the basics of her painting education—portraiture. She painted the portraits of her parents, often with tears in her eyes, over several days or weeks, and then, as a gift, mailed the canvas to whatever friend was in the picture. The joy and gratitude those friends of Viv's parents shared upon receiving their paintings started to breathe bits of life back into Viv.

When Viv's new condo was ready, the one she'd put a large deposit on during the first day of presales, she moved in on the first day she could. Typical Viv would've hosted an elaborate housewarming party filled to the brim with one hundred of her closest friends. But this was not typical Viv anymore. Other than movers and handymen, the only people who had ever set foot in her condo were Sylvie, Gabby, and eventually Zo. No one else was allowed. No friends, business colleagues, or female companions. No one. Ever.

Gabby, desperate to get Viv back into the limelight, suggested doing theme-based shows—Valentine's Day, summertime, Beyoncé's birthday—anything that would move the needle to get Viv's name on everyone's lips again. In that respect, it worked. People were excited to see Viv back, high-flying and entertaining them. Viv, on the other hand, was less than thrilled. She felt it was a cop-out and would rather not paint than become known for what she felt was too kitschy for her standards. She no-showed in protest to a few events and other public appearances, instead electing to spend time at a local watering hole and buy a round of drinks for the bar. Zo was hired shortly afterwards.

At her wits' end, Gabby quizzed Viv on what it was that she really wanted to do with the rest of her career: fold it up or get back to the top. Viv unequivocally wanted to get back to the top, but didn't believe her latest shows were the way to do it. Furthermore, she wasn't sure if getting back to the top was possible. Murmurs had started in the art world that she'd lost her magic touch. The more they grew, the more she believed them.

"Okay, so let's give 'em something to show that you've still got your magic," Gabby stated.

"Like what?" Viv had lost her confidence. In her mind, she had no story to tell. No point of view. No societal observation to spark her creativity.

Gabby urged Viv, with her hands on either side of Viv's head, "Dig deep. What's something you feel strongly about? Get into that big, beautiful brain of yours, unfreeze your heart, and find it. Just breathe. As your mom would tell you, it's in there somewhere."

Viv took a few deep breaths and quieted her brain to scan her emotions. After her parents' deaths, she felt numb to everything that had happened in her past and to the things happening in the present. She thought about situations, cultural events, and people in her life who had made an impact, but she still felt numb to all of it.

After turning over a few more stones in her head, Viv's eyes popped open. She was still angry and hurt that Ryan hadn't shown up at her parents' funeral, that she'd broken up with her without any explanation, and that she'd lashed out at Jack's funeral. That was enough to spark an emotional fire under her. "Okay, I'm in."

Gabby grinned. "There's my fighter."

In discussing the show, she also decided that it was time to debut the canvas tech she'd worked on with Henri; it was originally set to debut eighteen months ago. She worked to get herself back into shape, to eat regularly, and to become as social as she used to be. As much as she hated to admit it, having Zo did make life easier. Not only could she drink without worrying about driving or getting into a potentially unsanitary rideshare, she had more time to think through various ideas while he drove her from place to place.

Viv and Gabby worked tirelessly for two months to make sure everything was perfect for the show. The teaser press release. The arena. The paint. The sound system. The promotional art. *Immersive Love* was meant to firmly place Viv on the road back to the top of the art world. With the flip of a switch, the spotlight of fame returned brighter and hotter than ever before.

Chapter 14

Ladies Pavilion Sunsets

After Susana published her interview, it was game on. The love story of Viv and Ryan set the Internet ablaze for weeks. Gabby, in her signature style, seized every opportunity to keep the eyes on them. Outside of her shows and visits to her favorite watering holes, Viv had removed herself from both the art world and the general social scene ever since the death of her parents. Picking up women in the fashion she had been accustomed to for years was out of the question for the foreseeable future.

Gabby booked several photo shoots and sent them to every gallery opening, party, and high-profile event on the calendar. She'd discovered that Ryan was the only one Viv had ever let dress her, and she harnessed that trust and expertise to have Ryan shop for and curate Viv's style for each event. Viv's infamous fuck-it style was the one thing on which Gabby had never gotten Viv to budge. With Ryan in tow, this was her chance to introduce the world to an *elevated* Viv. The studio transformed into a production room to reconstruct the daily spectacle of a faux rekindled love, with which the media and the world became enamored. Each day ran like a well-oiled machine.

Zo would pick up Viv at her condo, her go-go juice chilled and already in the cupholder. She'd arrive at the studio, grab the ensemble of the day, change in the bathroom, retreat to the couch across from Ryan, and wait for instructions. She'd listen to Gabby run through details of the people who would be at the event, the people with whom Viv had lost touch, but who controlled several purse strings for art aficionados, the gossip magazine reps Viv hated but needed to make nice with, and other talking points for those interactions. Gabby would end each spiel with, "And remember, act like you love each other."

As much as Viv despised the situation she found herself in, she played ball. She was a natural charmer, like her mother, and she put on a fake face for both her artistic contemporaries and the general public. She'd boisterously share the story of how Ryan and she had met in the cafe and how she still couldn't believe she let Ryan steal her coffee. Ryan, for her part, was equally a good sport. It was impossible for those who came into contact with her to not see the creative genius and bold spirit hidden inside her demure disposition. She'd often make a complimentary comment on the construction of the garment worn by a guest or suggest a way to elevate a look for those who inquired.

It was their warm personalities that masked some of the shortfalls of their ruse. Viv was very deliberate in the way they expressed affection or PDA. They never held hands. There would be photographed instances where Ryan would lightly wrap her arm around Viv's, holding on to the inside of her sleeve, or with Viv nonchalantly draping her arm around Ryan, but making as minimal contact as possible. During professional photo shoots, she'd block out reality to get through the motions of staring into Ryan's eyes as she held her in her arms, laying her head on Ryan's shoulder on a balcony, or faking a smile while they playfully fed each other.

It was all business to Viv. As quickly as she turned it on, she turned it right off. Inside the car, there was never any conversation unless it was directed at Zo. As busy as Gabby kept their schedules, Viv was still going to *do Viv* at the end of the day.

Aside from the annoyance of the charade in general, she was worried about her ability to get her sex fix while being "in love."

Unbeknownst to her, the only thing more attractive than a famous artist was a famous artist who was taken. It felt as if only a few seconds after Susana's interview was published her phone started buzzing nonstop with calls from women she'd slept with last month, last year, and even as far back as ten years ago.

She'd had a glimpse of this strange dynamic before, when she was with Alana, but the situations were hardly similar. Being exclusive then was more of a progression than a declaration. While she had suitors text from time to time or lurk in her DMs, she ignored the advances because she was focused on one woman and one woman only. This was not that.

Ryan's reentry into Viv's life was loud and exposed. Viv went on record and said that Ryan was "the most amazing woman in my life." They were public in a way that Viv never cared to be with Alana. To the women in Viv's Rolodex, this presented a challenge they all were determined to overcome. In their minds, there was no way that Viv's behavior could change overnight and make her a one-woman woman. As for Viv, she went along with the illusion. If they believed that they could seduce her away from her "love" for just a few hours, that could only mean the sex would be fantastic.

She let the game come to her. Every night after a scheduled public appearance, Zo pulled into the garage of Viv's building and met another black Lincoln Navigator. Ryan exited Viv's car and got into the other car driven by Larry. He'd recently done six years in prison for petty drug charges and was eager to find work. Zo vouched for him, and Viv trusted Zo's word. Larry exited the garage first to take Ryan home, while Zo escorted Viv to the Intercontinental Hotel. They always arranged with management to provide access to the service elevator.

When they were in the hotel's parking garage, Zo handed Viv the key to the room reserved earlier in the day by Dylan. The reservations were made under a pseudonym and the name of Viv's guest for the night, who was instructed to pick up their key at the front desk and head to the suite to prepare for Viv's arrival. Dylan always staked out the room to make sure that no one else entered it. Upon Viv's arrival, Zo took over for the night.

Viv entered the suite to the customary bottles of champagne and small dessert bites in the main room, and she often found her guests lying across the bed or couch, or perched on the kitchen counter, in their best lingerie. The looks on their faces let Viv know they planned to bring their A games to that night's events. It was a time capsule of pleasure for Viv.

There was Sheila; they'd fucked on the floor of Viv's studio after one of her paint parties. Ana had fingered Viv in a movie theater when they were seniors in high school. The last time Viv saw Jordan, she ate Viv out while Viv stood with her naked body pressed against the glass of the Standard Hotel in New York after Viv had a show at Parsons. Candace taught the private pottery class Viv had enrolled in for fun postcollege. After three sessions, Viv had looked up to see Candace naked in front of her. Maddie she'd fucked on the docks of the Boathouse at Lake Merritt because the ten-minute walk back to her place was too long. Each one was a reminder of a time when she was carefree and fearless. Each one delivered mind-blowing sex to "remind you what's out there if you get bored."

Viv would stay in the hotel as long as she could before Zo would knock to signal that it was time to go. As much as Viv loved the blast-from-the-past sex, the return home to sleep alone was a stark reminder of the alternate universe in which she found herself living. She'd take a shot of whiskey and restlessly toss and turn in her king-sized bed, trying to sleep without a warm body next to her. She'd replay the night's events over and over in her head until her brain eventually shut off.

In order to further sell the illusion of being a real couple, when they didn't have a social gathering to attend, Gabby scheduled date nights for Ryan and Viv. They met Tuesday and Friday nights, along with an occasional Sunday brunch, at the most sought-after restaurants. Without the aid of others to fill the space, their conversation was nonexistent. The first few dinners were eaten in silence, aside from interacting with the waiter and asking each other what they were getting.

Gabby got wind of this from one of her colleagues who happened to be at the same restaurant. She stepped in and gave them scripted talking points to make it seem as if, at the very least, they actually *wanted* to be there. It all worked as long as everyone played their part.

Friday date night had arrived, and they had reservations at one of Viv's choices for once, Cafe Claude. It was a French restaurant in an alley of the Financial District. The staff that Viv was accustomed to had mostly moved on since the last time she'd visited, but the ownership had remained the same. The manager assigned their best server to their table, which was located in a cabana just outside the entrance.

Jo was a forty-one-year-old woman originally born in Romania. Her gaze met Viv's as she greeted them at their table. Viv took a full, unashamed look at her. She was striking at five foot nine with high cheekbones, light-brown skin, and long black hair slicked back into a ponytail. She'd lived in the US for twenty-two years, and although her accent was barely noticeable when she spoke, Viv picked up on it and coaxed her into sharing her backstory. She was still self-conscious of her English and over-compensated for it by being very gestural and expressive with her dark-brown eyes.

When Jo took their order, her fingers lingered over Viv's as she grabbed the menu and said, "If you need anything else, come find me." She gazed longingly back at Viv as she reentered the restaurant.

Viv followed Jo with her eyes and saw her slip behind a curtain, holding it open long enough for Viv to see that she had opened a door just beyond it. Viv took a few sips of her water while rubbing the back of her neck. She flashed a quick glance at Ryan and quickly blurted, "I need to go to the bathroom."

She casually rose from her seat and slowly made her way into the restaurant. She kept her head down as the servers whisked around her; the other patrons were engrossed in conversation. She poked her head behind the curtain and tried opening the same door.

Jo was waiting and reached for Viv's shirt to pull her into the tiny storage closet. There were boxes of inventory and shelving all around them, but Viv saw none of it. Jo locked the door and pulled her in for a kiss. Everything around Viv melted away. She was taken by the lust in Jo's lips and the heat of the moment.

She grabbed Jo by the waist as their tongues explored each other. She could feel the heat swelling between them as the wetness grew between her legs; Viv sensed the same was true for Jo. She unbuttoned Jo's slacks and pulled them down to her knees. Viv stroked her wet pussy through her soaked underwear.

Jo let out a soft moan in response and whispered, "I want your tongue."

Viv wasted no time. She leaned Jo against the small table and pulled her panties to her knees. She dropped to her knees and hungrily licked Jo's dripping pussy. Jo, working to keep her noise to a minimum, let out heavy gasps and bucked against Viv's face. Viv held on to her waist, moving in sync with Jo's reactions. Jo's hands were entangled in Viv's hair, pulling her in deeper. She felt Viv's tongue forcefully flicking against her clit in a circular motion before reversing direction. Each flick caused Jo to arch her back more and more, until she slid down the wall, her shoulders now on the table she was leaning on. Viv didn't miss a beat. She rose with Jo's movements, never deviating from her motions until she felt Jo's thighs tighten around her head and hold on while Jo's body convulsed, and her legs relaxed over Viv's shoulders.

As Jo gathered herself, Viv ran her fingers through her hair and wiped the juices off her face. Jo leaned in for another kiss before Viv attempted to go unnoticed back through the restaurant.

"Thanks for tipping your waitress," she said in a sultry voice.

With her eyes lowered, Viv replied, "Pleasure's all mine."

Viv slowly made her way around the curtain, through the restaurant, and back to her table. She attempted to play her extended bathroom trip off as she plopped back into her seat. "The drinks haven't come yet?"

Ryan, with her face flushed red, glared at Viv unamused. "You've got to be fucking kidding me. You're disgusting."

"What?" Viv was still playing as if she didn't know what the issue was.

"You fucked our server," Ryan said through clenched teeth.

Viv waved her off, crossing her arms and staring off into the alley. "You don't know what you're talking about."

"Your breath smells like pussy." Ryan composed herself in order to avoid a scene. Viv sat in her chair as if she were a kid who'd gotten caught stealing a cookie from the cookie jar. Ryan had no problem taking advantage of the silence. "You're so fucking unbelievable. I'm going along with this plan for *you*. You have this elaborate scheme to get your thrills, and you *still* have to color outside the lines. It's never enough for you, is it?"

Viv, annoyed by being reprimanded, leaned back in her chair and raised her eyebrows. "What would be enough for me is if you crawled back into whatever hole you've been in and left me the fuck alone. I don't need you to do this for me. I don't even know why you agreed to this in the first place."

"I'm doing this because I thought at some point you'd actually be open to hearing what I have to say. But I'm not going to be patient anymore. You're going to listen to me now, or I will blow the lid off this whole scam. You'll be the one with egg on your face. Not me."

That caught Viv's attention. *Fuck. Gabby's gonna kill me.* She sat up in her chair, tight-lipped, her eyes wide-open. She cleared her throat and gestured in Ryan's direction. "Okay. Well…talk. I'm listening."

"Not here. Tomorrow. Your studio, 8:00 a.m. Be there, or I'm *done*," Ryan declared with her voice slightly raised. She stood and threw her napkin down on the table before leaving. She couldn't trust herself to keep her cool if she saw Jo. More importantly, she didn't recognize the Viv she'd just witnessed.

Viv ate dinner alone before waiting at the Intercontinental for Jo, who was to join her to blow off some steam after she finished her shift. Later that night, after stumbling to her place, Viv received a flurry of texts.

Gabby: What is this I hear about trouble in paradise?

Gabby: How long of a leash do you think you have here?

Gabby: You can NOT blow this.

Gabby: Fix it! ASAP.

Viv rubbed her eyes; she had dozed off in her living room. She kept her responses short and sweet.

Viv: Okay.

Viv: I will.

Viv: Chill. I'm going to bed.

Chapter 15
Pineapple of Hospitality

Sporting an oversized black hoodie and dark-gray sweatpants, Viv dragged herself to her studio at 7:51 a.m. that Saturday morning. She sleepily rolled up the doors to let the light in. Watching the sun streak across the brushed-concrete floor in complete silence would normally be her favorite part of the day. She'd bask in it, stretching her arms above her head before grabbing a canvas and painting her heart's desire of the moment. She'd sketch out plans for a new idea or do research for an upcoming show. Despite her reliance on music as her calling card, it was during the quiet moments in the studio that her brain experienced peak performance.

This morning was far from that. She let out a deep sigh as the roll-up door hit the top of the track. She sipped on her usual smoothie and sat in her director's chair, facing the door and waiting for Ryan's arrival. Her left knee nervously bounced up and down. She tried to slow her breathing, but her anxiety grew steadily with each passing second.

God, I look like shit. How did I end up here? What if she doesn't come? What if this is another test? Why do I even care how she feels? Fuck, I hope she doesn't come.

She had no idea what to expect from Ryan. They'd only had one conversation in twelve years—at Jack's funeral—and that was a shit show. She checked her phone incessantly, watching the analog second hand of the clock icon rotate, both willing the time to move faster and simultaneously wishing time would stand still. Her heart beat faster the closer the clock ticked to 8:00 a.m.

Ryan's shadow appeared, approaching the door as the clock ticked to 8:01 a.m. Viv was so tense she felt as if she were sitting on a chair of needles. Ryan slowly opened the door and slipped inside. She was wearing a nondescript green fatigue shirt underneath a black cardigan and skinny blue jeans. She looked as if she had been crying.

Ryan's solemn mood was a far cry from where it was the night before. She wished she had talked to Viv then when she had the benefit of blind rage to give her the courage she needed. In the fourteen hours that had elapsed since, she'd admitted her feelings for Viv, and then she'd ended up back in her head, unsure of where to start.

She cleared her throat and walked halfway to where Viv was seated. "You came."

Viv nodded. "You told me to."

The silence between them was deafening. Viv rested her right arm on the armrest and leaned her forehead against her fist. Ryan nervously fidgeted with her pockets and avoided eye contact. She'd lost all of her words and nerve. Though she'd forced Viv's hand with an ultimatum, at this moment, she desperately wanted to do nothing but disappear.

Viv began to grow tired with this charade. "Is there something you wanted to say?" she asked dryly.

"Yea...I...ugh...ummm..." Ryan sighed, frustrated with herself as more silence filled the room.

Viv moved her from anxious to irritated. "Fuck, Ryan. What the hell is this? Did you just want to see if I'd show up if you asked?"

Ryan shook her head before drawing a sharp breath. "Your show," she said softly, "it was about me. Us."

"Yeah, sure. Keep telling yourself that." Viv fanned off the assumption.

"Vivi, you used to play that Etta James song every Sunday morning when you'd make us blueberry pancakes. You know my favorite color is lavender, and you used all blues and lavender."

Viv sat forward with her elbows on her knees, her temper growing. "Do you think this is *The Da Vinci Code*? I don't need you to decode or interpret my art for me."

Ryan pressed a bit further, "Vivi...I...I didn't realize how much I hurt you, or how much it still affects you. I really wa—"

Ryan didn't get to finish. Viv had heard enough. "Is that what this is about? I don't need your fucking pity! You have a lotta nerve, you know that? You fall off the face of the fucking planet for over a decade, and then you show up out of the blue and turn my life inside out. I was doing perfectly fine before you showed up." She got up out of her chair to walk towards the door. "This is bullshit. Don't stand here and act like you're doing me any fucking favors. You left *ME*, remember?"

Ryan stammered in the face of Viv's rage, "I...just want you to understand..."

"Understand what?" Viv walked past Ryan to leave.

Ryan grabbed her arm as she passed. "HE BEAT ME!" Ryan took a couple of steps backward, panting wide-eyed while she caught her breath.

Viv's rage dissolved into confusion and concern. "Wh-what are you talking about? Who are you talking about?" she asked with a furrowed brow.

"Jack"—Ryan's eyes met Viv's—"the night that we got back from the ceremony. When he received his award, I told him that I was planning to move to San Francisco a few years after graduation. He asked me why I'd want to move to a city full of fags. I don't know what came over me, but I was tired of hiding. I told him that I wanted to move to one because I was one too, and I was in love with you.

"I'd never seen him so angry or speechless before. He stared at me with such a look of disgust, for what felt like forever, and then the next thing I knew I felt his hand slam across my face, which knocked me into the bookshelf. He kicked me so hard in the ribs I thought my lungs were going to pop out. I remember crying in pain, coughing blood up onto the carpet while he paced around the living room. He screamed that no kid of his was going to be a fag. I tried to stand when he rushed over to me, the award still clenched in his fist. I put my hands up over my head to defend myself as he barreled over to me, raising the award. The last thing I remember seeing is this look of pure hatred in his eyes from in between my arms."

Ryan paused, rubbing the scar on her forehead. "The next thing I remembered was waking up in the hospital. He'd brought me in himself and told them I'd been mugged. When I came to, he was there with my flip phone in his hand. He stood over me and forced me to send that text to you. After I sent it, he snapped the phone in half. He apparently told the hospital that I had suicidal tendencies, so they held me for seventy-two hours for monitoring." Ryan lowered her eyes as she hung her head; they raced back and forth as she stared at her feet.

Viv stood frozen in shock as Ryan connected the dots that had always eluded her. When Ryan arrived home from the hospital, Todd was waiting in the living room. Todd's dad, Ted, was in the same platoon as Jack. Ted had previously shared with Jack during their poker games that his son wasn't the sharpest tool in the shed and that he didn't want to support a freeloader if he couldn't keep a job. Jack, who previously was never interested in Ryan's life, became obsessed with it. Jack used his connections to land Todd a highly sought-after, entry-level role at one of New York City's top REITs. In exchange, Todd agreed to date Ryan and keep her away from any *"faggot behavior."*

Jack flatly told Ryan that she'd be seeing Todd from then on. When she objected, Jack told her that her options were to comply, or he'd break her legs and send her to conversion therapy. After she finally nodded nervously in agreement, Jack instructed Todd to take her to her room to consummate their relationship.

She and Todd had known each other since childhood, casually growing up in the same church, and he had never been a mean person. Behind the bedroom door, she pleaded with him that he didn't have to do what her father said.

His response, "Money and pussy on a platter? I'm set for life." The pressure of Todd's weight on top of her, crushing her severely bruised ribs, was a memory that still haunted her.

Ryan's life faded to black-and-white from that day forward. She was given strict orders to interact only with those on campus who were deemed necessary to her education—professors, classmates for a group project, and school administration. Todd escorted her from campus to her apartment every day and checked her texts and calls once inside, quizzing her if there was a number or name he didn't recognize.

Upon graduation, they were wed in a small backyard gathering. Her life with Todd was far from the union she'd dreamt of with Viv. Jack deemed that women need only exist to serve their husbands, but you have to throw them a bone here and there. Ryan dreamt of continuing to build her fashion brand, but instead she was allowed to apply to entry-level positions at companies that solely produced male clothing. When her friends went on trips, she wasn't allowed to go and always came up with a convenient excuse. Eventually, the invites stopped altogether.

Given that Ryan hadn't shared that she had her tubes tied in college, Todd tried fruitlessly to have children. She pleaded with her doctor to keep her secret. As a result, Todd's apathy and indifference towards Ryan grew. On his good days, he'd get drunk and sleep with other women. On bad days, he'd come home and slap Ryan across the face for being a "worthless barren bitch." With Todd less focused on her every move, when he would go away on business, she'd venture into the city to visit the gay bars. It was those brief hours that gave her a bit of respite. A taste of freedom. Occasionally, she had the courage to flirt back with a potential suitor and slept with a handful of them over the years.

She thought her life would never be her own again until, suddenly, Jack died. Her personal boogeyman and tormentor was dead. She was free. Almost. She spoke with Todd about a divorce, but he refused. By then, he'd fathered several children with another woman, and though he never loved Ryan, he had come to enjoy the power he held over her. Despite the rise in social media after college, she never reached out to any of her old friends because of the shame and embarrassment she felt.

At the funeral, she had a pivotal private moment with Sylvie in which she asked if Sylvie's uncle could help Ryan get out of her marriage.

Sylvie agreed to help without hesitation. She and her uncle took care of everything Ryan could've asked for. They filed a restraining order against Todd and housed her in an apartment in the city. After several months of preparation and negotiation, they agreed on terms and were ready to finalize their divorce. Sylvie flew to New York to support Ryan in the final proceedings. They were together when she received the news of Geraldine's and Henri's murders. Sylvie urged Ryan to attend the funeral, but after the debacle at Jack's, she believed that it would be better for Viv if she wasn't there.

After the divorce was finalized, she quit her job and moved to LA. The California sun kissed her skin in the mornings for her runs, and she felt glimpses of true freedom. She'd lost over a decade of her life, and her self-esteem and self-worth in the process. At Sylvie's suggestion, she began to see a therapist twice a week to unpack, process, grieve, and address the hell that she experienced. After a year of therapy and self-reflection, she made the decision to move to San Francisco in hopes of reconnecting with Viv. Though they had no contact, she'd followed her career, reading every review and admiring the photographs of her gallery and work.

Once in San Francisco, acting on that desire proved harder than she'd imagined. She attended all of Viv's themed shows, sitting in the back row in a black hoodie and shades. She watched Viv fly through the air and saw the same Vivi painting furiously in their old apartment. Each time, she told herself that she'd approach Viv at the after-party, but she never did. She'd either slip out immediately after the show or watch Viv get swarmed by people and become overwhelmed. The *Immersive Love* show touched Ryan in a way that gave her the most courage she'd ever had.

"When I heard the chords for 'At Last' begin to play, I knew this story was about us. About you and the pain I caused you. I know I shouldn't have interrupted your show, but I felt if I didn't do it then, I never would. I want you to know that I never stopped wanting you, and I never ever stopped loving you."

Viv stood motionless as every word escaped Ryan's lips. Desperately wanting to cover her ears and shut them out, but equally hurting and unsure of what she could do.

Ryan took a big breath and chose her next words carefully. "Listen, I know you hate me for breaking your heart. And for the way I acted at Jack's funeral. But probably, most of all, for not showing up to pay my respects to Geraldine and Henri, who loved me like I was their own daughter. But…Vivi…before all of that happened…we were friends. Do…? Do you think we can be friends again?"

Viv, still a statue, with tear-filled eyes, nodded. Ryan's eyes rose from the floor to meet hers as Viv cracked the faintest of smiles. Viv's voice cracked as she spoke, "Can I give you a hug?"

Ryan nodded quickly. As Viv walked towards her, the tears Ryan had held back began streaming down her face. "I'm so sorry, Vivi." Ryan gripped the back of Viv's hoodie as she sobbed openly in her arms.

Viv held on as tightly as she could, holding the back of Ryan's head, her fingers entangled in her hair. "It's not your fault, Ry. It's not your fault," Viv whispered into her ear as she slowly rocked Ryan in her arms.

Chapter 16

Ferrari Bombs

They stood in the studio for what felt like an eternity. With Ryan in her arms sobbing, Viv's mind was spinning, unable to process it all completely. The years of anger she'd felt towards Ryan melted away as she squeezed her tighter. She felt her shirt getting wetter, pressing against her skin as Ryan's tears flowed freely. She'd spent so much time trying to figure out what could have happened to break them up. So many drunken hours trying to forget her. She'd convinced herself after Jack's funeral that if she *never* saw Ryan again in her life, it would be too soon. Now, she found herself wishing that she had done something back then to help her. Wishing that she'd fought harder.

Through her tears, Ryan felt a weight finally lift off her shoulders. As much as the life she'd lived pained her, what hurt her the most was that she never had a chance to tell Viv the truth. For years, she watched Viv photographed with different women on her arm and wondered if, underneath all of that, she was truly happy. If she still thought about their love. If she still cared. If she still believed in love at all. The Viv she knew was deeply focused on finding her one and only, but maybe fame had changed that. Changed her. Now, in her most vulnerable moment, she found solace in Viv's arms. Her head rested on Viv's shoulder as she slowly regained her composure.

As her breathing became more regular, Ryan dropped her arms from around Viv's waist, took a small step back, and wiped her tears. She took a deep breath, stalling while she tried to figure out how to navigate the vulnerable state in which they suddenly found themselves.

"Do you want to get some air?" Viv asked, breaking the tension. "Maybe go for a walk?"

"I'd like that, yeah." Ryan cracked a small smile at the suggestion.

For the first few blocks, they walked in silence through the SOMA district that surrounded the studio, both unsure what to talk about after such a heavy moment. The sun poked through the morning fog as the wind blew lightly. The streets were relatively empty at this hour, until someone on a Lime scooter sped by them.

"A lot has changed since the last time I was here," Ryan said, breaking the silence.

Viv agreed and explained the events that led to the transformation of the city. She noted the huge number of young tech workers who lived in San Francisco and commuted to Mountain View, Menlo Park, or Santa Clara for work because, to twenty-two- and twenty-three-year-olds, there wasn't anything appealing about a sleepy suburb. The City of San Francisco had taken note and responded by giving tech companies multiyear tax breaks in exchange for signing leases for new offices within the city limits. Twitter was the first to make the move to a building on the corner of Tenth and Market.

That was the first of many office relocations and expansions that accelerated the wave of gentrification, not just in SOMA, but in the Mission District, Nob Hill, Tenderloin, the Financial District, and the Marina. Those neighborhoods were all greatly affected. The Tenderloin was a place consistently riddled with homeless people and drug addicts. Because of that, a few years ago you could find a sizable one-bedroom apartment for around $1,000, give or take, depending on the building. Now, even though the homeless problem had only been exacerbated by gentrification, that same apartment was $3,500. Viv considered herself fortunate as she was able to buy her studio before the prices soared to unattainable levels for both the artist community and the general working class. It had become a city for the rich, and while Viv was "one of those people" now, it depressed her to see the city lose so much of its magic.

They walked down Folsom Street towards Embarcadero Street, which hugged the Bay immediately to the east. They stopped briefly at Philz Coffee to grab a couple of their specialty coffees and pastries before continuing their walk to the water. Once on the Embarcadero, in front of them was the bow-and-arrow sculpture, *Cupid's Span*, by one of Viv's favorite artists, Claes Oldenburg. He was famous for creating larger-than-life structures of everyday objects. Most people would recognize the *Giant Binoculars* in Los Angeles or *Needle Threading a Button* in New York's Fashion District. Of all the art in the city, this was Viv's favorite. With the Bay Bridge as a backdrop, the strings of the bow mimicked the suspension cables of the bridge and brought to mind Tony Bennett's song "I Left My Heart in San Francisco."

Viv hailed a pedicab to take them up the Embarcadero to Fisherman's Wharf.

"Vivi, what are you doing? You're paying forty bucks to go less than two miles? We can walk that in like twenty minutes."

Viv plopped herself into the seat of the pedicab and tapped the seat for Ryan to join her. "Nah, this will be faster."

"What happened to the New Yorker in you?" Ryan jokingly chastised.

"She got a black card," Viv quipped back, casually draping her arm around Ryan once she reluctantly took her seat. "Is this okay? I don't know why I did that."

"No...no, yeah. It's fine. It's nice." Ryan smiled back as she reached up to give Viv's hand a gentle squeeze. Her face turned serious as she pointed in Viv's direction. "You can never tell anyone I took one of these stupid things," she said gesturing at their transport.

"Your secret's safe with me, Pearce," Viv replied as they began their ride.

The conversation between them had become easier. They traded smiles and laughs as they people-watched and made witty commentary on their short journey. Once at the Wharf, they continued their walk. Engrossed in conversation, they moved down Jefferson Street, passed the souvenir stores bursting with trinkets, laughed at people getting scared by the famous Bushman, and braved the fish market that overwhelmed your nostrils, no matter how many times you experienced it. When they reached In-N-Out Burger, they paused to grab fries and milkshakes before continuing their walk.

They strolled through the San Francisco Maritime National Historical Park on the walkway adjacent to a little beach that led to the bay. Ryan shook her head in disbelief that people still willingly swam in the water when everyone knew about the water's high mercury content.

Viv laughed in agreement. "Some people are gluttons for punishment." They made their way into the Presidio. Formerly an outpost for housing military families, it had been turned into a public park with historical museums and recreational spaces that included a bougie country club and golf course.

Ryan's pace was a step too quick for Viv. She considered herself very physically fit, but they were five miles into their walk, and she was shocked at how quickly Ryan made her way through the winding trails. Feeling competitive, Viv mustered up all her energy to make her way past Ryan.

"Ah, I see you *DO* still have a little New Yorker in you," Ryan yelled as she quickened her stride to keep pace. They eventually reached the Sand Ladder at Baker Beach on the northwest side of the city. The Sand Ladder is a long, winding decline that goes down to the beach. They made their way down the oversized sand stairs that required you to take two to three steps forward before reaching the edge of the next step. The stairs were flanked by vertical logs, wires running through them that acted as guardrails. They removed their shoes halfway down as the sand wasted no time infiltrating them. Once on the beach, they walked eastwards to a small cove where there was a bluff of large rocks. They carefully made their way up and over the rocks, finding their footing, until they reached a flat portion where you could sit comfortably.

On more days than not, the fog was so dense that you couldn't see across the water to the North Bay or Golden Gate Bridge to the right of the rocks. Fortunately, on this day it was barely cloudy, with a thin fog belt running just over the top of the bridge. The wind whipped across their faces as they sat; the water below crashed against the rocks, splashing them lightly. They paused to watch the tour boats passing underneath the bridge in the distance.

"Had enough?" Ryan said, teasing Viv.

Viv shook her head and replied with a smile, "Nah, I've got like five more miles in me." Truth be told, she was tired, but with the conversation flowing between them, she'd hardly noticed.

Ryan bent her head backwards, feeling the sun through the breeze. "I remember when you first brought me here that one summer, and we had to walk through the nudist section of the beach."

Viv laughed. "Ha! I remember that. You were mortified and worked so hard not to look. I remember wanting to take you here because it felt similar to when we'd go to Williamsburg and sit on the rocks at the East River. It was one of our favorite things, remember? Grabbing a bite, sitting near the water, talking shit about New York, and bitching about college, our goals for adulthood... Simpler times..." Her voice faded as she stopped speaking.

The deafening silence returned. The wind picked up, causing the waves to roar louder as they crashed on the rocks. Ryan had a thousand thoughts running through her head, but didn't know how to respond or where Viv's mind was. Luckily, Viv clued her in.

She turned towards Ryan. "Let me get this straight. You swore Sylvie to secrecy, and you agreed to this...this whole fake relationship thing...just so you could finally tell me what happened all those years ago?"

Ryan shrugged her shoulders and nodded. "If that's what it took, yeah. I hadn't really thought past having the courage to approach you."

"Wouldn't it have been easier to tell me the truth when Gabby brought you to the studio the day after the show?"

Ryan raised her eyebrows. "Would you have listened? Honestly?"

Viv sighed, staring back at the water with her lips pursed; then she turned back to face Ryan. "No. Not a chance." She sat and pondered further, tapping her knee as she went into a trancelike state. She held her knees close to her chest, rocking rhythmically back and forth. She gazed far off in the distance.

Ryan, remembering Viv's bouts of deep thought, remained quiet, watching the waves until Viv broke out of her reverie.

"So, now, what do we do? You told me. I listened. Do we need to continue this fake relationship?"

Ryan shrugged. "I mean, it doesn't bother me, if that's what you're asking."

"It's not what I'm asking." Viv squinted and held the bridge of her nose before continuing, "I'm sorry. I'm not thinking straight. Let me try again. You agreed to all of this, I'm the only one who benefited from it, and I've been an asshole to you this whole time. How can I help you now?"

"Vivi, I don't need anything from you. Really, I'm fine."

"Come *on*, Ry," Viv urged, shaking Ryan's shoulder and making her sway side to side. "There has to be something you want. Just be selfish. For once. Please?"

Ryan looked down at her feet, moving side to side, her lips pressed tightly together, until she parted them to respond, "Well… there is this one thing I'd love to show you."

Viv gestured with her hands for her to continue.

Ryan pulled her phone out of her pocket and tapped for a while before holding it tightly against her chest with both hands, elbows out wide. "Don't laugh, okay?"

"Okay."

"Promise?" Ryan asked, wide-eyed.

"I promise."

Ryan scooted closer to Viv and started to explain as she swiped through photos. "I've followed pretty much every show you've done, read the reviews, and archived photographs of your work. I obviously wasn't present to see you paint them, but I saw you do it all the time in our old apartment, so I could see the passion and emotion of each brushstroke.

"At some point, while Todd was away on a business trip, I got the idea to trace over the photographs on my iPad. I found different silhouettes on each canvas. I got a little too excited and wondered what it would look like if I recreated *your* art with *my* art. I took the outline from each canvas and sketched a look. Taking into consideration the colors, themes, and depths of the brushstrokes, I came up with these."

Viv grabbed Ryan's phone to get a closer look. She zoomed in on various sketches and high-fidelity renderings. She saw work from over a decade ago, as well as her recent pieces. Ryan had created everything from evening dresses to casual wear, pants suits, swimsuits, and everything in between based on Viv's paintings. The colors on the canvas were translated into accent additions for each look, boldly slashing across and through an otherwise-elegantly-designed garment.

Viv flipped furiously but curiously through each design and each piece of art until she came across a pair of outfits. They were contemporary robes designed for a male-female couple. The robes were fitted with sleeves that flared out at the ends and pants that tapered in at the calf. Each featured gold draping and had streaks of dark blue and orange that were meant to connect if you placed the robes side by side. Viv zoomed in and out, looking at the details of the rendering. She tapped the image to display the file name. Geraldine and Henri. Viv looked up in astonishment at Ryan, who was half biting her lip in anticipation.

"What do you think?"

"This is"—Viv paused to rub the front of her nose and compose her thoughts—"this is incredible. I'm kind of speechless. You definitely haven't lost your eye."

"I know it's kind of a strange hobby, but it was one of the few things that kept me sane for so many years. Designing these reminded me of who I used to be. It gave me hope in the same way that designing did in high school. Hope that I'd one day be free to be who I wanted to be. Anyway, I haven't gotten around to photographing them all yet, b—"

"You've actually constructed these?" Viv asked, her interest and excitement level rising.

"Some of them, yeah. They're at my studio in Berkeley."

"Can we go see it now?"

"Sure," Ryan said through a faint smile, "I'll call us a car."

Viv remained silent as they climbed down the rocks and entered their ride when it arrived. She didn't know what to make of the past twenty-four hours, but instead of questioning it, she elected to ride the high while it was here.

When they arrived at the studio, Ryan was suddenly embarrassed. She paused before entering. "It isn't much, but this is it," she said, pulling the cord above her head to light up the space. She stood with her hands in her pockets as Viv scanned the room.

The studio was barely 400 square feet, and Ryan had utilized every possible inch. She had her worktable and sewing machine in one corner, her fabrics rolled up against the opposite wall, and the mannequins filled the center of the space. Her sketches covered every inch of the cork-covered wall panels. There were easily over a hundred ideas splattered across the walls. The space may have been physically small, but to Viv, it felt massive as Ryan's creativity dominated. It was a museum of Ryan's mind, and Viv wanted to admire every artifact. She looked at the garments that Ryan had constructed from her sketches, rubbing the fabrics between her fingers gently and cherishing the intense craftsmanship that was Ryan's signature.

"They're over here," Ryan said, moving a Japanese folding screen to reveal the mannequins that featured the Geraldine and Henri designs. "I keep them separate so they don't get messed up by any of my other work. It gets pretty chaotic in here sometimes." She stepped aside as Viv came closer.

Viv ran her hands along the sleeves of one design, stroked the draping on another, her fingertips tracing over each detail. The big brushstrokes that crossed the chest of both patterns brought her back to the pain of that show, her parents' funeral proceedings, and the agony that followed. She fought back her own tears and turned to face Ryan. "Has anyone else seen them?" she asked between deep breaths.

"Nope. Just you. But I would like to share them somehow, if that's okay," Ryan replied, tempering her word choice because she recognized that Viv was in a vulnerable state.

"It's more than okay. I'll get Gabby and the team working on this, no problem. We'll handle the cost and logistics to put on a proper show. Whatever you want. You can have it," Viv enthusiastically replied.

Ryan smiled from ear to ear. "Vivi, thank you so, so much. It really means a lot to me."

Viv waved her off. "It's the least I can do. You have so many amazing ideas on these walls. I'm overwhelmed by it all." She placed her hands on her hips, scanning the space that was clearly hindering Ryan from creating all of her visions. Her mind hadn't stopped racing since they left the beach. She stood in place, leaning from side to side, pushing her mouth from one side of her face to the other, before she spun around with excitement. "You need more space to create! Why don't we make space for you in my studio? I can get you a key made, and we can rearrange where I store my canvases and where the team builds different arrangements. You'll have more than *triple* this size that can be all yours."

Ryan held back her excitement. "That's really generous of you. Are you sure I wouldn't be cramping your style?"

"I'm positive. That's what friends are for, right?" She lightly patted Ryan on the arm.

Ryan stared at the ground and took a breath before looking back up with a smile. "Right."

Chapter 17

Frozen on a Balcony

"You know, Viv, when you fuck up, you *really* fuck up. But when you deliver, boy, do you DELIVER!" Gabby grabbed Viv's cheeks with enthusiasm, as if she were the aunt everyone dreads seeing.

Viv glanced over at the monitor on Gabby's desk and saw multiple windows open. Each one featured photos of her and Ryan out and about the city yesterday. Walking side by side downtown. Viv pointing out sights to Ryan in the pedicab. Both of them staring intently out at the bay. The headlines ranged from somewhat amusing to downright cringeworthy.

San Francisco's Favorite Couple

Just a Blip on the Radar?

Gay by the Bay

Sittin' on the Dock of the Bay…In Love

Knowing she was trapped in Gabby's clutches, Viv recoiled inside. She had always been a reluctant celebrity. She never really considered herself better or more important than anyone else, even though long before she was famous, her magnetism was felt every time she walked into a room. She always said yes to signing an autograph, taking a selfie, and showing up where she was told. Absent of that, she was largely unaware and unfazed by cameras or onlookers in her day-to-day life, as was the case on her day out and about with Ryan. That said, she was well aware that she was constantly being written about in the media or talked about by the masses. For mental-health reasons, she did her best to stay away from social media after the death of her parents. Her accounts were managed by Gabby's team, and she usually only knew she was trending if a friend sent a screenshot of tweets, or more likely than not, Gabby would incessantly text updates when there was a media mention.

Gabby finally released Viv's cheeks and took a step backwards. "How did you go from almost ruining a good thing to having an unscheduled day date?" she asked.

"It wasn't a day date. We were just hanging out." Viv moved to walk past her.

Gabby grabbed her arm and looked her in the eyes. "So you had sex then? Yes?"

Viv sighed. "We didn't."

"So how'd you get her back on board?"

"We talked. Well, she mostly talked. I listened, and now things are fine. End of story," Viv replied nonchalantly.

"Just when I think I've seen it all, you surprise me, kid," Gabby said, smiling and patting Viv on the shoulder. "Come on; we've gotta review the show schedule again."

"Sure, but first we need to make some changes in here," Viv replied, pointing to the studio.

History felt as if it were repeating itself. Similar to when Ryan moved into their apartment in New York, Viv's studio made a transformation that rendered it unrecognizable, even though the remodel was her idea this time around. Although Viv never complained, she secretly hated that there was a lot of wasted space in the studio. The luxury of space allowed ample opportunities to be messy and chaotic. To make room for Ryan, that would have to change.

The canvases were now neatly stored along the wall, instead of piled on top of each other. The workshop was freed from the various scraps left over from previous projects or old unused ideas. The tools were moved off several desks and stored on shelves along the rear wall. Viv's desk, still a three-by-five table with a canvas screwed onto its legs, was placed against the wall that separated the studio from the arena, which was across from Gabby's team.

To the left of Viv's desk was Ryan's new studio space. Her mannequins ran the length of the wall, her space was separated from Viv's by only the large corkboard with Ryan's ideas and sketches pinned to it. She had a sewing station and four large tables that made a six-by-ten workspace for her to make the patterns necessary for her designs. Large rolls of fabric were suspended both above the mannequins and on the bathroom wall that jutted out into the studio.

Viv's crew handled the transportation of Ryan's materials from her previous studio and set everything up exactly to Viv's specifications as she was hyperfocused on making the space "just right." She relied on her memory of their apartment to recreate the environment in which Ryan thrived. She had them look up articles from Ryan's previous shows when they were students at Parsons; they were hung on the walls to give Ryan a sense of ownership, inspiration, and pride in the space.

***

Viv nervously waited for Ryan's arrival at the studio once she deemed the space good to go and texted Ryan to come check it out. She paced back and forth before Larry arrived and escorted a blindfolded Ryan out of the car. Viv held on to Ryan's shoulders as she walked her into the studio. "Okay, are you ready?"

Ryan eagerly nodded as Viv anxiously fumbled to untie the blindfold. Ryan was speechless. She beamed from ear to ear upon seeing the amount of space that Viv had dedicated to her. "Oh my gosh! I have so much...SPACE!" She held her arms out wide before leaning over the large tables, basking in happiness. "Thank you, Vivi. This is perfect."

"No problem. I'm glad you like it." With her nervousness subsiding, Viv felt a sense of relief. Though she couldn't erase the pain in Ryan's life, she knew she could help create a safe haven, a fresh start for her.

"I love it!" Ryan replied, springing up off the table and into Viv's arms.

"Okay, okay, okay, are we done with the HGTV moment?" Gabby interjected. Inside, she was happy for Ryan too, and while it was a breath of fresh air to see Viv self-motivated again, she needed her to focus now that she'd completed her pet project. "We have work to do, people!" she said as she clapped her hands and walked to the schedule board.

Although the studio remodel made the biggest impact on Ryan, the change of scenery was not lost on Viv either. You could argue that she'd become complacent. She'd been coming to the same space for over a decade, and it suddenly felt as if new life had been breathed into it. She felt it in the creative energy flowing through the space, as much as she saw it in the physical changes. She'd never minded being a lone wolf or working in silence with her ideas, but with Ryan in the studio, her imagination and capacity for new projects began expanding rapidly.

It felt as it had during the simpler times in their apartment, which relaxed Viv. Suddenly, she didn't have to be a walking brand. She was just Vivi. She'd often come into the studio to find Ryan cutting patterns or making modifications on a mannequin, her mouth full of pins. Viv would sip her vodka-infused smoothie while Ryan showed her what she was working on, wide-eyed with pens in her hair, like a mad scientist. She'd play an '80s and '90s playlist over the arena speakers as she continued with her work, while Viv settled in at her desk to answer emails from vendors, past buyers, and fans. They sang along in harmony to all of their favorite songs. Off-key, but harmonious nonetheless. It was infectious.

When Gabby's team and the crew arrived, it turned into a full-on sing-along for twenty minutes before they had to cut it out so they could start their phone calls for the day. To the team, it seemed that Viv was much easier to be around. She'd been fortunate to have very low staff turnover over the years as they certainly loved her and would never have said that she was a bad boss. But there was an intensity that came with working for her. Every move, every decision, even where their materials were sourced—you could see in her eyes that she treated her work as if her life depended on it. In Viv's eyes, it did. With sex and alcohol as her chosen life partners, she'd stopped being Viv the Person and only walked through life as Vivienne Roche the Brand.

Since she and Ryan had spoken, Viv's intensity meter had been dialed back a few notches. She had more patience. She would sleep on things and reassess the next day, instead of obsessing on them overnight and unveiling a grand plan first thing in the morning.

As for Ryan, she was warm and friendly with everyone and had no problem winning them over. They loved her easygoing personality almost as much as they admired the garments she was producing. Her creative prowess was impossible to miss, which, in turn, made it even easier for Gabby to build initial buzz around the upcoming fashion show that Viv had promised her. That would have to wait a bit.

Gabby had already sold *Vivienne Roche: The Love Series* to several media outlets. The world unanimously loved Viv being in love, and they wanted more of the same. This presented a challenge for Viv because, aside from her themed shows, she typically saw each show as its own production, its own vision, its own stand-alone world.

She expressed her frustration to Gabby once she heard the news. "This doesn't make any sense. A series? What are they expecting to see here? This isn't a Broadway musical."

"They love your heart! Your raw emotion. You know, when you stop being Viv the Artist, who is untouchable, and become *Unmasked* Viv, the everyday person that's struggling like everyone else," Gabby continued, trying to sell her vision to Viv, but with little success. She looked at her artist, who was staring blankly back at her, thoroughly unimpressed.

Viv opened her mouth to speak. Closed it. Tapped her foot. She thought for a moment longer before deciding on her response. "And what am I supposed to do with that? Break my own heart every night?" She held her hands together on top of her head as she stared vaguely at the ceiling, shaking her head.

"You're *Viv Roche*. You'll figure it out. You always do. I've got calls to make, kiddo. Let's pick this up later." Gabby gave Viv a slight pat on the arm before walking to her side of the studio.

Viv, unable to comprehend how she could make this work, walked briskly outside to smoke a cigarette. It was a windy morning, the sun poking through as morning fog gave way to light cloud cover.

Ryan was coming out of the bathroom when she saw the exchange between Viv and Gabby. She contemplated following Viv after she left in a huff.

Gabby advised against it. "Better to let her blow off steam than get burned for caring."

***

Viv leaned against the gray concrete walls as she fumbled to retrieve the cigarettes from her pocket. Once in hand, she flipped open the pack, tapped it, and grabbed one of the remaining cigarettes with her mouth. She took a long, slow drag once it was lit and closed her eyes, letting out a deep sigh in the process. Opening her eyes, she watched as the fog mingled with her smoke.

Fuck. Now I've backed myself into an impossible corner. Just when I think things have taken a turn for the better, I still end up with no control. What am I supposed to do with a series? Come on, Viv, think!

Viv's thoughts were interrupted by the sound of the ringing church bells at Saint Patrick Church. She walked in the direction of the church, staring at the ground and continuously running into roadblocks while thinking of how to work inside the confines Gabby had given her. Saint Patrick's was a brick church from the 1800s that had survived both the 1906 and the 1989 earthquakes. It stood directly across from Yerba Buena Gardens, a man-made park that sat on top of the underground portion of the Moscone Convention Center. Surrounding the park was MOMA to the north; Yerba Buena Center for the Arts, the theater at YCBA, to the west; and AMC's Metreon movie theater to the south.

Viv knew this area like the back of her hand. Geraldine had several shows here; Viv had exhibited and performed in these spaces on several occasions, and she'd come here to admire the work of many of her contemporaries. Long before the world knew her name, Viv had come to the park with friends, lain in the sun, or watched free shows at the small amphitheater.

Her favorite feature was one of the signature standouts of the park—the waterfall. The roaring of the water was audible from the sidewalk. What made it special was a small pathway that allowed you to walk behind it. Inside of the carved-out space, etched into the stone, were quotes from several of Dr. Martin Luther King's speeches. It was a powerful display and tribute that she and her parents frequented when she was a child. Back then, she stood in awe of having words so important that they were eternally engraved into stone. As an adult, returning to it always brought Viv peace.

She turned at the center of the walkway to stare out at the park. The water obscuring her view. The mist grazing her arms, the roar of the waterfall the only audible thing. It drowned out the sound of her thoughts. She took a few more deep breaths as she watched the water land in the contained pond before it was recirculated back to the top.

She slowly made her way out of the exhibit and took the concrete stairs, which flanked either side of the waterfall, to the second level. This level was much quieter; there was a thin, eyebrow-shaped pond that used the same recirculated water; benches lined its entire length. To the rear was Samovar Tea Lounge and a beautiful trellis with chess tables; you often found locals deeply entrenched in games.

She sat on one of the benches for another hour. Despite the serene environment, her mind raced the entire time. She'd never had an issue creating visions for her shows, even when they were commissioned for an event or by special request. She could not, however, wrap her head around this one.

Viv nervously bounced her leg before jumping up swiftly. She walked a couple of blocks to the 7-Eleven on Market and bought another pack of cigarettes and a beer before returning to the studio. The wind whipped against her face. She fought against the gale with each step she took, which made her journey back even more dreadful than it already was. It was as if the world were trying to give her a sign to run in the other direction. Reluctantly and begrudgingly, she trekked forward.

***

Back at her desk, Viv took long sips of her beer and painted on the canvas in front of her with a small brush. She had a special small easel she'd received as a kid that she kept for this purpose. She'd painted countless times with this same setup, usually when she was working on a new concept, before presenting it to her team for commentary. In this instance she was painting mindlessly, as if in a state of hypnosis, still trying to find a solution.

"I take it you're not thrilled about the *Love Series*?" Ryan poked her head over the top of the canvas. She'd been in a meeting with Gabby about the fashion show when Viv returned to the studio.

Viv broke out of her trance to look up at Ryan with puppy-dog eyes. "Please don't tell me you're on her side too."

Ryan walked around the canvas and grabbed a stool to sit on the side of the table. "I'm not on anyone's side. It's not an argument. It's art."

Viv sat back in her director's chair, poking at her bottom lip with the back of her thin paintbrush. "I can't repeat a show, Ry. Or even the same story line. If I was doing a residency at Vegas, then sure. But these are brand-new shows where I'm expected to regurgitate the same concept."

"You're wrong, Vivi. You don't have to do that at all."

Viv scratched her head. "How do ya figure?"

"Gabby's selling a love *series*, not a love *story*." Excited, Ryan raised her eyebrows.

Viv wasn't following. She scrunched up her face. "Is there a difference?"

"Of course. Art has multiple interpretations. I mean, I don't have to tell you this, but your big, beautiful brain is not seeing that right now. So I'm going to explain this like we're in intro to art class. Did you ever consider that a love series doesn't have to be about people?"

Viv took another swig of beer and interlocked her fingers in front of her face, as confused as she was intrigued. "What would it be about then?"

"What do you love? Not including your infamous 'Sex, alcohol, and art' mantra," Ryan said with a smirk.

"Very funny." Viv took a deep breath as she stretched her back, her arms reaching above her head, before slouching back into her chair. "Shit. Um, growing up in the Bay Area, drag, traveling, the '90s, New York…food…um, I guess working out too."

"So then, make your shows about THAT. You're the artist. If they're in love with *you* being in love, then show them *all* the things and places you love. Except working out. No one cares about that."

Viv stared at Ryan intensely for several moments, processing her statements carefully, but ignoring her sarcastic remark. Without warning, she sprang up in her seat, grabbed a paper and pencil, and began sketching furiously for a few seconds before turning to Ryan. "Okay! I have an idea."

Ryan smiled and leaned in to hear more.

Chapter 18

Radio City

Once Viv had presented her vision, Gabby wasn't thrilled with the direction in which Viv was going in. In her words, she "didn't get it," but there was no denying that the fire in Viv's eyes was back. "Viv, are you sure about this? I can sell with the best of 'em, but do you think people will be moved by this?" Gabby was leaning on her desk and holding her right fist with her left, both pressed underneath her lips.

"As sure as I've ever been. For *Big Apple Love*, we can fly to New York to do a show in the city itself. I was thinkin' we could do it at the Astor Place Cube. It's not far from our old apartment. It's outdoors, so it'll be a bit more tricky and hella expensive, but I think it'll be great. Also, why don't we bill Ryan's show as the finale of the *Love Series*? What better way to close it out, no?"

Both Viv and Ryan laid the theatrics on thick to sell the essence of the show. In the end, it wasn't the idea that sold her. It was the electricity she saw between the two of them. That electricity she could harness and sell to the masses. If she killed the idea, the electricity would die with it. No electricity, no eyeballs. No eyeballs, no dollars. When they finished their spiel, she quickly agreed as if it were the best idea she'd ever heard. Viv would continue to take off her metaphorical mask and show what made her tick, her influences on full display, starting with her love of the region that raised her.

Gabby leaned back and rocked in her chair. "Vivienne, you keep this up, and I'm gonna be out of a job soon. I love it! I knew you'd figure something out. Don't start booking your own interviews now too."

"And torture myself? No, thank you. You're the grown up here." Viv smiled, satisfied that the strategy worked.

"Yes, yes. You give me so many reasons to remember that fact. I couldn't *fathom* forgetting," she joked. "Now scram. I've gotta get on the horn to sell this new direction."

***

Viv spent the next few days ruminating on what a show about her hometown should be about. There were so many possibilities. She called up Sylvie one afternoon to get her opinion.

"Romeo, Romeo. Nice to hear from thou, Romeo," Sylvie joked.

Viv rolled her eyes. "Fuck off. I have a serious question, dude. Growing up here, what's something that stood out to you? The thing that could only happen to us growing up in the Bay, you know?"

Sylvie thought about it for a few moments. "Shit. That's a hard question. There's so many things."

"Right!" Viv shouted with her free hand outstretched as she paced. "How can I even deconstruct the anatomy of the Bay, simplify it to one thing, and then set it to music?"

"Actually"—Sylvie paused—"*that* is the thing. Remember, in college, we'd listen to a ton of Bay Area rappers our friends had never heard of, and we'd go on and on about the Hyphy Movement. How it didn't matter what city you were from or what race you were. Everyone just vibed."

Viv replied smiling, "See, THIS is why you're on the team." Sylvie was right. It was perfect.

"Awwww, now tell me you love me," Sylvie joked.

Viv rolled her eyes again. "Goodbye, idiot."

"Close enough. *Ciao*, lovebird."

***

Old habits die hard. The day of the show, Viv's traditional intensity returned. She didn't arrive as early as usual, but she still wanted to review everything, do a test run, and review everything again. After the test run, she asked the foreman to make a change on two of the paint ledges. She sat in the far corner of the arena with Ryan, watching them make the adjustment.

It was around this time that members of the media arrived to get set up; in addition, her VIPs were allowed early entry to get settled in and receive their complimentary beverages. They usually never saw Viv preshow, as any adjustments needed and another test run were completed well before the doors opened.

At thirty minutes before showtime, the general public started to trickle in. On cue, Zo appeared with a tray holding three filled glasses. "Boss, your usual go-go juice—pineapple and tequila," he said, handing the drink to Viv. "And for you, Ms. Ryan, I have the options of Topo Chico or a sparkling rosé for you to choose from."

Ryan turned to Viv, flashing a smile. "My favorites. You remembered." She was visibly blushing.

"Remember? How could I forget? We had so many bottles that ate up prime beer real estate in the fridge, not to mention the amount of times you asked me to go to that specialty-foods store to buy more on my way home."

Ryan, still smiling, returned her attention to Zo. "I'll take the Topo Chico today, please, Zo. You can have my wine."

"No problem. Here you go, Ms. Ryan," he said, handing the glass to her before making his way back into the studio.

"Cheers," Viv said, raising her glass slightly and then putting it to her lips. Before she could get a taste, Ryan intervened, stopping the upward motion with her hand, their fingers grazing each other's in the process. Viv looked at her in bewilderment and simultaneously felt a spark fly up her arm.

Ryan lowered her voice to just above a whisper and said, "I know you think you need this to handle your anxiety, but I don't think you do. I've seen you do it a million times in our old apartment, completely sober. You've got this. Just take a deep breath. Quiet your mind."

Viv stared back at Ryan as if she'd seen a ghost. She was tight-lipped, and doubt shone clearly in her eyes.

Ryan continued, "Here. Let's switch for tonight." She took Viv's drink and replaced it with hers. "Cheers."

"Cheers." Viv was still spooked by the idea.

Ryan sipped hers first and licked her lips in approval. "Mmph, this is delicious. I can see why you like this," she said, nodding her head. "Much better than all those Long Islands you used to order. Your turn."

Viv took a sip of the flavorless carbonated water and scrunched up her face in disgust. Her tongue moved in and out of her mouth as if she were a dog that just ate peanut butter. "Good God, I forgot that this tastes like ass."

Ryan giggled at the sight. "I guess you forgot that part. To be clear, I meant what I said about your anxiety, but your face was the cherry on top."

Viv shook Ryan's knee with her hand. "Jerk."

They laughed together as if they were schoolgirls without a care in the world. The sounds of cameras clicking and lights flashing soon followed as the media feverishly tried to capture every moment, hoping to catch that elusive public kiss.

The foreman walked over to give his report, obscuring the reporters' views in the process. "All done, Boss. Let's get you ready to go."

***

To start the show, Viv walked to the corner of the arena floor in the dim lighting. This wasn't the starting point that people were accustomed to, nor was she wearing her usual outfit. Instead of an all-black, full-body leotard, tonight she was a vision in all white. She shook her hands trying to calm herself. Her go-go juice always provided a slightly fuzzy layer to mask her nerves, but she didn't have that luxury today. She took a deep breath and prayed that Ryan's intuition was right.

Before the lights went up, the set list started. The lights came up as the bass and track of the Federation's "Go Dumb" blasted through the speakers. Viv grabbed her opening paintbrushes out of their canisters and ran into the arena in a frenzy, jumping up to give herself initial flight, before her crew steadied her motions. Her strokes matched the freneticism of the track as the canvases were splattered with neon green, orange, yellow, and magenta. At times, she'd land on the ledges or drop back to the floor and dance to her favorite parts of the song.

The challenge with this show was there were no slow, ethereal moments that had become her signature. This was hyphy music. Everything was up-tempo, which meant that Viv's energy level had to keep up with the pace of each song. She rarely had gas left in the tank during run-throughs, but Viv refused to cut a song from the set list. She claimed that removing even one wouldn't do the Bay music scene justice.

You wouldn't know that she'd struggled getting through the set during rehearsals. In this moment, Viv looked as if she could've done the show twice without breaking a sweat. She danced her way through Messy Marv's "Get on My Hype," Mac Dre's "Feelin' Myself," another Federation song, "Hyphy," the Pack's "Vans," JT the Bigga Figga's "Game Recognize Game," Digital Underground's "Humpty Dance," and the Luniz classic, "I Got 5 on It."

Viv's painting was always unpredictable, but her dancing tended to have a loose structure that changed depending on either the type of feeling she wanted to evoke from the audience or the theme if it was a special show—salsa, Viennese waltz, line dancing, and so on. There was none of that present in the *For the Love of the Bay* show. It was pure joy.

She interacted with the audience during the Auto-Tuned portions of Nump, "I Gott Grapes," mouthing the words, swinging back and forth between two ledges, and then dropping back to the floor. She continued through the final tracks, a smile never fading from her face during E-40's "Tell Me When to Go," embodying all of the dance moves and facial expressions, before closing out with a theatrical version of Too $hort's "Blow the Whistle." Viv waved her arms above her head and pointed at the audience as the lights cut out on the final line.

The crowd roared in applause. The lights came back up quickly as the Team's "It's Getting Hot" began to play. Viv continued dancing on the floor of the arena before running across it and up into the bleachers, dancing with the audience. She ran back down, stopping in front of the VIP row, waving her arms up and down to get them onto their feet. She ran back to the arena floor and beamed at the crowd that was having just as much fun as she was. She jumped up, landed on her back on the arena floor, and sprang back to her feet. She signaled to keep the music going before waving to the crowd and running backstage.

Backstage, a wide-eyed Viv ran her paint-covered fingers through her hair, taking deep breaths to calm her heart rate. She couldn't tell if her heart or her mind was in overdrive. All she knew was that her body felt alive.

Zo, who was ever ready in his usual postshow spot, extended his arm in her direction. "Go-go juice, Boss?"

"No, no. Not yet anyway. I want to bask in this feeling a little bit longer," Viv said, panting with her hands on her knees.

The room was abuzz when Viv emerged from her postshow shower. She entered the after-party to find Ryan's eyes locked on her; she was waiting with a big smile and a glass of champagne. Once Viv took it, Ryan placed her fingers to her lips and emulated a chef's kiss. *Fantastico!*

Viv, matching Ryan's gaze, opened her mouth to respond, but Gabby interrupted, "You were right, Viv. The energy in this room is nuts. We need to capitalize! You and Ryan go schmooze. Go! Go!"

***

The media was in a frenzy about the New Viv. Her fans, known as the V-Hive, were ecstatic to see her happy again. Maybe the happiest they'd ever seen her. In baseball, when a hitter is hot, there's a phrase that is used: the game has slowed down. It refers to being in the zone, to when an athlete is at peak performance. That's how it was for Viv. Art became easier. In fact, everything became easier.

The scheduled date nights became less of an obligation and something to which she looked forward. Ryan and she spent the majority of the time sketching on napkins and taking pictures with anyone who wanted one. Viv picked up her regular nights at TOP again, but this time with Ryan by her side. They'd sit in her usual booth, with Sylvie joining them on most nights. The three amigas were more than enjoying the reunion. They'd huddle around the table doing shots, reminiscing, playing drinking games, or just simply enjoying each other's company.

The photo shoots Gabby booked felt less awkward. Before, Viv would avoid any suggestion that Ryan and she look directly at each other. Now, they'd easily become locked in a stare, even after the photographers indicated they had a good shot. They found themselves in the studio late into the evenings, both throwing out a million ideas, just as they did in college.

"I'm getting hungry. Do you want Chinese tonight?" Viv was intensely staring at her computer when Ryan broke their creative silence. "Vivi? Vivi, are you hearing me?"

Viv slowly began turning her head as she furiously typed away on her laptop and clicked the touch pad. Then, she fully faced Ryan and said, "Huh? What's going on? Sorry, I had to finish that email. I hate seeing draft emails laying around in my in-box, so I have to hit Send before I can do anything else. Did you ask me something?"

Another Viv-ism. Ryan laughed to herself about Viv's endless quirks. "I asked if you wanted Chinese tonight for dinner?"

"Yeah, that sounds goo—" Viv's phone buzzed on her desk. A mischievous smirk crept across her face before she grabbed her keys. "Uh, actually, Ry, I kinda have to go somewhere. Like right now. You understand, right?"

"Yeah. Yeah, of course. Go do your thing. I'll close up here," Ryan said as nonchalantly as she could.

"Awesome. Thanks. Text me after Larry drops you off, so I know you made it home safe."

Viv headed towards the rear exit to her car as Ryan sighed behind her, plopping back down on her stool. *Ugh, I'm so stupid. Of course, she has plans. This isn't your old apartment. You're not REAL girlfriends. You're just girls that are friends. That's it.*

Ryan knew that she and Viv both thoroughly enjoyed their arranged-date nights, their impromptu hangouts off-the-clock, and creating together again. In their minds, it gave them both a welcome breath of fresh air and a new lease on life.

Ryan's presence made Viv's working hours and daily life a breeze in a way she hadn't felt in years. But that was only half of the equation. Despite all that, Viv was still gonna be Viv. Her DMs and texts from past flames never ceased lighting up her phone on a day-to-day basis, and in turn, she saw no reason to stop answering them. The happier she appeared, the more her suitors desired to deliver great sex. The only shitty part of her life that had remained constant was sleeping alone; she bought a top-of-the-line body pillow to make it less dreadful.

Viv had the glow that most would say came only from being in love. For every interview, she made sure to attribute the glow to being reunited with Ryan. Behind the façade, Viv knew her glow was obtained through amazing sex. Those closest to her couldn't deny that Viv was definitely happier, but they weren't sure if they should believe the façade and Viv's words or the reality of her actions.

Chapter 19
Stolen Kisses at the Flagpole

"Are you really in love with this girl?" Belle asked as Viv's head poked out from underneath the sheets on her king-sized bed.

"What?" Viv, pretending she'd not heard the question, continued to lay a slow trail of kisses from Belle's belly button up to her neck.

Even as Belle swayed her body back and forth in pleasure, she remained unswayed in her train of thought. "Are you actually happy when you're with Ryan?" she said, rephrasing the question, placing both hands on Viv's shoulders. "Like…*really* in love?"

Viv looked down at Belle, her flowing hair covering the gray-silk pillowcase on which her head rested. Her blue eyes stared intently back at Viv as if she were looking into her soul, trying to yank the answer out since Viv seemed to have no interest in giving her one. Viv, relying on her sexuality, leaned down, planted a soft, passionate kiss on her lips, and stroked Belle's face lightly. "Is this *really* what you want to talk about right now?" she asked in a sultry voice.

Belle moved from underneath Viv to lie beside her and turned on her side, propping her head up on her fist. "Yes. It is."

Viv tried to joke her way around the topic. "Geez, was I that bad? Or are you jealous?" she said with a smirk.

Belle wasn't going to entertain Viv's antics as she returned the smirk with a blank stare. "You're stalling. And deflecting. Answer the question. You know you can trust me."

Viv sat up straight, tapping her thumbs together as she leaned against the light-gray, upholstered headboard. She sighed. "Fine. I'll answer, but why are you asking?"

"Because"—Belle looked up at Viv and maintained intense eye contact—"at first I thought it was some staged BS that Gabby cooked up since she's kind of a neurotic, opportunistic genius." Viv raised her eyebrows and nodded at the description as Belle continued, "I figured it would dissolve in a week or two, given the public's attention span. But now, you *actually* look like you're enjoying yourself. So naturally, given that you're still sleeping with me and countless other women, no doubt, I'm curious."

"Curiosity killed the cat," Viv quipped.

"You already did that," Belle joked. She was one of the few people who could keep up with Viv's rapid-fire banter. "Now, answer me."

"Well, you're right. *Immersive Love* was the one show that I knew would finally shed the naysayers about the future of my career, and it went perfectly. Until Ryan crashed the ending. That cannibalized the reviews of the actual show, and before I could even wrap my head around it, Gabby waltzed her into the studio to sell this fake relationship."

Viv paused, staring straight in front of her. She tilted her head back and took a slow, deep breath before continuing. "I hated it. Hated her. I fought against it. And then I kind of fucked up and was forced to finally listen to what Ry had to say. And it changed…everything between us. I'm not gonna put her business out there, but she experienced and put up with some really, *really* terrible shit for so long. Knowing that the person I once loved more than anything had experienced that kind of pain and restriction. It hurt like hell hearing it, but I finally understood. After that, the tension and anger was gone. We've just been having fun. As friends."

Belle nodded, taking in Viv's words. "And what is she getting out of it? Besides an overnight high-profile public persona, verified on socials, and an all-expenses-paid fashion show?"

Viv shrugged. "Honestly, I don't know. She said it doesn't bother her."

"So when's the fake wedding?"

Viv brushed her off. "Don't be ridiculous."

Belle pressed, "I'm serious. Just because she said it doesn't bother her doesn't mean that other things don't bother her. Or that, I don't know, maybe she has her own wants and dreams? I don't know what happened with her, but I get the sense she didn't have much say in the way her life unfolded. I'm not saying you're a bad person or treating her unfairly, but you should be careful you're not recreating a less horrific version of whatever it is she went through. Even if she's enjoying your company, and vice versa." She paused before giving Viv's hand a light squeeze. "Just think about it at some point, okay?"

"Okay." Viv sat quietly, stunned by Belle's comments and insights. She nodded her head slowly before agreeing. "I'll think about it."

"Great!" Belle, still full of energy and satisfied with the response she'd received, flung herself over to the other side of the bed and straddled Viv. "Okay. Where were we?"

"Hold on," Viv stopped her from leaning in for a kiss, "Since we're having actual conversations today, I have a question for you."

"Oooh...quid pro quo. Seems fair. Go for it." Belle leaned back, resting her ass on Viv's shins, and gestured with her hands for Viv to bring the proverbial heat.

"What would you have said if I said that I was actually in love with her?" Viv said while squinting.

Belle smirked and patted Viv on her stomach. "Viv, you're a fantastic lay, so I'd miss that. But my answer? I would ask you what the hell you're doing with me or any of these other girls if she really is the one. I'm selfless like that," she said, flashing a cheesy smile afterwards.

"Selfless enough to let me ask you one more question?" Viv quizzed, leaning forward.

Belle shrugged nonchalantly, biting her lip. "Dealer's choice. It's gonna cost you though."

Viv pressed on, "My painting. I still don't know how you have this. Was it a gift?"

Belle shook her head.

"You bought it yourself? At a show?"

Belle nodded. "Also...that was three questions."

"That's impossible. I write thank-you notes to all my buyers and donors, and I've never written one to you. I even went back and looked at the buyer list from that show, and there's no Belle listed. I host private parties for my VIPs from time to time, and I've never seen you at one of those. I'm not saying you're not rich because"—Viv gestured with her arms at Belle's condo—"obviously you are. What I'm saying is, I don't understand how you, Belle, bought it if there's no record of it."

Belle smiled slyly, hiding her own nerves and rubbing her hands up and down Viv's arms. "Oh, Viv. Your anal retentiveness is showing. That's an easy answer. You don't know me because you don't remember."

"I remember everything," Viv retorted confidently.

Belle rolled her eyes, undeterred. "Does the last name Antanasijevic mean anything to you?"

"Antanasijevic?" Viv repeated in order to confirm the name.

Belle nodded, her hands self-consciously balled into fists. She scored the insides of her palms with her nails while she waited for a response.

"Antanasijevic, Antanasijevic, Antanasijevic." Viv scanned her mental Rolodex. "I only know one person with that name. She was a one-time buyer. Her name was Mirabelle Antanasijevic."

"Otherwise known as Belle?" Belle asked.

Viv tilted her head slightly to the left.

"It's nice to see you again, Viv," Belle said while smiling.

Viv looked puzzled. "How did I not put that together? It's so simple."

"Maybe because you blocked out flirting with me at your after-party," Belle said matter-of-factly. "It was for a show you did at Parsons after you graduated. You went to call a car to take us to the Standard Hotel, but you never came back. I guess someone else must've stolen your attention."

Viv's eyes widened at the retelling of the story. "Um, I'm…sorry."

"Don't be. You're the one who missed on this bomb sex that night," Belle joked. She caressed Viv's shoulders before she rubbed her fingers up against Viv's clit. "You know, people get things wrong at times. Even you, Viv."

Chapter 20

300-Percent Tip

Vivienne Roche: The Love Series was a smash hit with critics and fans alike. Viv's effervescence captivated anyone who witnessed one of the seven shows in the series, which started with *For the Love of the Bay* and ended with *Ryan's Love*. Each show had its own unique signature, revealing more and more of what made Viv *the* Viv that everyone adored and knew very little about, outside of her very carefully manicured public persona.

The second show was *Born Naked and Loving Drag*. Her set list was composed of singles from drag queens who'd appeared on *RuPaul's Drag Race*, as well as local San Francisco queens. For Viv, it wasn't enough to just have the music. In order to pay proper tribute, she booked each featured queen to perform simultaneously on a special stage built to be elevated above the arena floor, where Viv's primary large canvas would normally hang. She envied the queens for being unapologetically themselves, in spite of what the world may think. Outside of her shows, Viv was still learning how to do this in her day-to-day life.

A World Full of Love featured songs from or about her favorite countries around the world and incorporated traditional dances from each location. Each paint station featured the colors of one country's flag, and the after-party featured the quintessential cuisine of all the countries featured in the show. Growing up, Viv had always been adventurous and curious about how the rest of the world lived. She understood the privilege her adult life afforded her and wanted to share a bit of her experiences with her fans.

The Love of Geraldine and Henri: A Reprise was a much more intimate look into Viv's childhood. With her emotions controlled this time, home videos of her and her parents over the years played above the center canvas. Conquering her fears, she opted to use oil paint as a tribute to her mother, using the techniques that Geraldine showed her as a child. The techniques were fuzzy in Viv's head, as she hadn't practiced them in almost two decades. Unafraid to be messy and imperfect, she was able to maintain her composure *and* feel joy, displaying the pure magic of the love they had for her and each other. It was a welcome reprieve from the deep, stabbing ache she felt when she dwelled on their memories.

Big Apple Love was the much anticipated New York City show. Viv was correct that it was going to be tricky and extremely expensive to pull off in such a public place. For protection, the Astor Cube was covered by a larger cube which featured promotional material for the show. The makeshift arena was pushed as close to the building that the plaza opened to as possible, so there would be space for people to gather and for the onlookers in the main plaza, in the smaller plaza across the street, and in the side street.

Viv always enjoyed performing in the city she referred to as her second home. This was no different as she watched hundreds of people react to the set list, singing along to Jim Jones's "We Fly High (Ballin')," vibing out to Nicki Minaj's "Beez in the

Trap," or belting out the song that started Viv's meteoric rise to fame: JAY-Z and Alicia Keys's "Empire State of Mind" with their famous New York City pride. The pure joy and elation that she felt as she flew through the air in the same neighborhood that the young, wide-eyed, broke, aspiring-artist Viv had lived in was immeasurable. Out of the corners of her eyes, she could see people in the windows of the historic stone and brick buildings that surrounded Astor Place. At some point, she thought she saw people on rooftops. Though she couldn't hear it with her headphones in, she was sure there were cars honking at the surprised drivers who'd stopped temporarily to try and figure out what was going on. It made her laugh inside that she was now the cause of the incessant New York City noise that she'd complain about in their old apartment.

She'd done countless shows in New York, but this one was special. It seemed to spur a desire to exorcise a few additional demons. One thing that had constantly bothered Viv for the majority of her career was that only the wealthy could afford her real paintings. For this show, she decided to break the mold and incorporate a raffle of several canvases, one foot by one foot, for free to spectators. The smiles on the faces of the raffle winners, when Ryan called their numbers, stayed put while taking a photo with Viv and their new painting; for Viv, it was a drug that felt better than all of her drunken sexcapades combined. The typical after-party and schmoozing was replaced by a block party, for which a DJ kept the music going for hours.

Viv found Ryan once she'd met with the last raffle winner and changed out of her performance attire. "Phew! This is…this is somethin', isn't it?"

"Yeah!" Ryan replied excitedly. "You really made a lot of people's day, maybe even week with the raffle and free show. It's always good to let the world know you've still got plenty of tricks up your sleeves."

Viv smiled and opened her mouth to reply, but just then her phone started buzzing. She pulled it out of her pocket to check the messages and raised her eyebrows to their highest point in surprise and excitement as a devilish smirk made its way across her face.

"Need to go?" Ryan asked, trying her best to pretend she didn't know that Viv had just received a sext.

"Uh…" Viv looked up at Ryan, saw the disappointment on her face, and hurriedly sent a text before putting her phone back in her pocket. "Nope. I'm all yours. Let's get out of here before Gabby spots us."

Ryan beamed at Viv's reply as they walked arm in arm, leaving the party behind, and headed on a stroll through the Lower East Side with Zo and Larry walking a comfortable distance behind them. They grabbed a bite at their favorite place, Empanada Mama. They scarfed down several of the fully stuffed and fla-vorful empanadas before coming up for air. They recalled their college years when they'd go to the old hole-in-the-wall location in Hell's Kitchen at four in the morning after partying all night. People would file into a space that was barely three feet wide to get their order in. Once their order was called, they'd sit on the stoops of neighboring brownstones and inhale the food, praying it would soak up all the alcohol in time for their classes.

Zo left briefly to retrieve the car and returned to drive them across the East River to Williamsburg, where they sat on the same rocks as they did fifteen years ago. Once they were settled, they sat in silence as the warm summer breeze caressed their faces. It was always amazing that from this view, looking out at the city, the city that never sleeps, it seemed completely still. The river softly splashed against the rocks below them, filling the silence.

Viv tilted her head towards the sun, basking in its warmth. "I've always wanted to do something like what we just did. Make art truly accessible. Not just for the one percent."

"So why haven't you?"

Viv paused and squinted out across the water. "Eh. It's Gabby. She always felt like it would dilute my '*brand*.'" Viv used air quotes, illustrating her irritation with the concept.

"Fuck that!" Ryan exclaimed. "Your *brand* is you being yourself. Raw. Authentic. You're the artist. An artist that's not desperate for money, at that. Worry about what brings you joy, not how much press Gabby can drum up for you. Trust your gut."

"Yeah. I guess you're right." Viv nodded, still staring across the river and taking in Ryan's words.

The silence returned for a few minutes before Ryan broke it. "Do you ever think about what would've happened if we didn't break up? I mean…if I wasn't forced to break up with you?"

Viv inhaled sharply through her nose. "No. Not really. Not anymore, at least." She exhaled slowly. "Back then? Yeah. I thought about it all the time. But it hurt too much, so I shut it down. Pushed it out of my head."

Ryan moved her leg and tapped Viv's knee with it. "Can you tell me what you thought about, at least?"

Viv tilted her head left to right a few times before answering, "We would've been happy, I imagine. Maybe adopt a kid or two. A dog, for sure. Game nights with my parents. Traveling the world and desperately, maybe naively, trying to change it through art. But…you can't rewind time." Viv paused before adding, "You would've been the bigger star though. You always were. You still are; the world just hasn't seen it yet. But in a few weeks, that'll change, and they'll all see how brilliant you are. That's one thing that can still happen."

Ryan felt her heart warm by Viv's words, but she didn't know how to respond or where to start. "A dog, definitely. I always thought you'd make a great mom. You learned from the best. And I don't doubt for a second that we would've been happy." Ryan paused briefly to make sure she didn't start rambling. "Look at us now. I never thought I'd get the chance to see you again, let alone laugh with you. In the city that made us. Brought us together."

"The same one where you stole my coffee." Viv grinned.

"Ladies and Gentlemen, the Golden Grudge Award once again goes toooo…Vivienne Roche!" Ryan exclaimed, pretending to hold a microphone in one hand and to hand the invisible award to Viv with the other.

Viv's body stiffened as her tone became serious. "I need to tell you something."

Ryan's smile faded when she noticed the shift in Viv's demeanor. She placed her hand on Viv's right shoulder. "Okay. What is it?"

Viv took a deep breath before exhaling. "I went to your house."

"What? What house? How? When?" Ryan was confused, her heart rate rising.

"After you sent the breakup text. I called and called, but it went straight to voice mail. I printed out the directions and took the train to a friend's place and borrowed his car. When I got to your place, Jack answered the door. I told him who I was, and he told me you weren't home and that he didn't know when you'd be back." Viv's voice broke as she struggled to find her words. "When you told me how he reacted to you coming out, I...I feel like maybe I... Did I make it worse...like the whole Todd thing was—"

"Oh, Vivi." Ryan rubbed her back lightly. "You had nothing to do with what he did. Nothing. And there's nothing that anyone could have done to change it. I always thought that maybe if I'd kept my mouth shut, everything would've been fine, and we would've lived happily ever after. But Jack was a terrible human that would've found a way to make things miserable, no matter what we did." She leaned her head against Viv's as she spoke.

"So much for happy," Viv said, letting out a sigh. "Ry. I'm sorry I let that text stop me from making any effort to connect with you over the years. I just spent *so* much time hating you. I grew up so idealistic about love, and I was sure I'd found it with you. Your text broke me in a way I still haven't been able to fix."

Ryan draped her arms across Viv's bent legs. "I'm sorry I wasn't brave enough to reach out to you or anyone about what was actually happening. You hear stories like this, but you never think that something like that could happen to you, you know? Todd made sure that I was either isolated or under constant supervision. I couldn't make choices for my career, for my body. I felt like I was trapped in an adult version of my childhood that I'd tried so hard to shed in college. The confidence I'd built in those three years faded into oblivion. I constantly felt like a deer in the headlights, frozen. It was all so...embarrassing.

Humiliating." Ryan hung her head down and held her hands in her lap, shifting her fingers at random.

Viv placed her hand on top of them. "It's over now, RyRy," Viv said softly.

Ryan's ears perked up at the sound of her old nickname.

Viv continued, "He's off doing what the fuck ever, and you are free to be happy. On your terms. Find someone that will stop at nothing to make you feel valued, loved, and respected. You deserve nothing less."

They locked eyes, acknowledging the vulnerability that was shared between them. Their blossoming bond, though severed for over a decade, was palpable to any onlookers. They were so lost in their own world they didn't hear Zo approaching.

"Boss, it's Gabby. I have to get you back to the hotel, so we can get you both ready for tonight's gala."

Fuckiiiing Gabby.

They nodded in acknowledgment and took one last look at the water, as if they were bidding their former dreams a final adieu before heading back to reality.

Chapter 21

Twenty-Three Minutes Late

They returned to San Francisco for the final two shows, *The Love of a Liar* and *Ryan's Love*. Riding high from *Big Apple Love*, the general public impatiently waited for the sixth show before the focus shifted from Viv and rested squarely on Ryan. The titles of the preceding five shows offered the audience an idea of what to expect. Ryan chose the cryptic title *Ryan's Love* since this was her debut redo. It was a nod to the fact that no one knew anything about her, what she was passionate about, or what drove her. If they wanted answers to those questions, they'd have to show up and find out.

When covering Viv, who everyone knew was a perfectionist, the media assumed they'd witness shows that only focused on her high points since she desperately repressed and forcibly forgot any failures. The subject matter of each show surprised both the spectators and her inner circle. For her sixth show, *The Love of a Liar,* she once again took them all by surprise, addressing the one thing she'd never publicly commented on in the two years since it happened—her breakup with Alana.

The ease that she felt around Ryan in recent weeks brought Alana back to the forefront of her mind. Along with that came questions she'd never asked herself before: Was she ever really in love? Were there red flags she should've seen? She'd spent her whole life not caring what other people thought, but at the time Alana and she met, watching her friends get married got to her somehow. What was worse, it twisted her away from her instincts so much so that she didn't even consider that her parents had legitimate concerns about their future daughter-in-law. She remembered Geraldine's mantra, "Love doesn't need excuses."

When Viv was in a full-on depression spiral in the aftermath of her parents' funeral services, Alana quickly pounced to attack her character, saying that Viv was narcissistic, that her drinking caused her to be verbally abusive, and that she needed "home training." Despite the fact that a small amount of the general public took the bait, a PR statement was never made, and Viv herself never addressed it. Her engagement was a failure. Her love was a failure. Her judge of character was a failure. And up until recently, Viv blamed herself for things happening the way they did.

Was there a new Viv? She certainly saw things with fresh eyes. It wasn't like Alana was very private about her views back then; she called Viv's art a circus routine right before they slept together in the studio. Although Alana knew what she was doing from the start, she pulled the wool over Viv's eyes in a way that made it feel like true love. Instead of continuing to view their relationship as a failure, Viv wanted to celebrate that they never made it to the altar. Despite the mental and emotional journey that the breakup caused, she had to admit that she was still happier than she would've been under the spell of a liar. The time to remain silent was over.

Viv pulled no punches when it came to the set list. She came out swinging with Ying Yang Twins' "Naggin'," before guiding the crowd through Kanye West's "Gold Digger," Beyoncé's "Sorry," Bell Biv Devoe's "Poison," OutKast's "Roses," CeeLo Green's "Fuck You," Alanis Morissette's "You Oughta Know," Bon Jovi's "You Give Love a Bad Name," Pink's "So What," the All-American Rejects' "Gives You Hell," Bruno Mars's "Grenade," and Eamon's "Fuck It (I Don't Want You Back)," before closing it out with Justin Timberlake's "Cry Me a River."

Her approach was a stark contrast to *Immersive Love*, in which she was, though unplanned, more demure in the beginning and unrestrained by the end. In *The Love of a Liar*, she came out guns blazing and slowly became more refined, cerebral, and concise in her emotions as she got deeper into the set list. *Immersive Love* featured different hues of blues and lavender. *The Love of a Liar* featured hues of red, black, and white. As "Cry Me a River" slowly faded and Viv was lowered to the floor, Alana's face was projected onto the canvases. Viv greeted them by flashing both middle fingers before waving goodbye. Once on the floor, she didn't do her customary bow and bask in the applause. Instead, when she landed with her back to the audience, Viv unclipped herself from her harness, walked backstage without making eye contact or speaking to anyone, and headed straight for her shower.

As the heat of the water ran over her skin, she leaned her forehead against the shower tile. She rarely thought of Alana anymore, but the show had unearthed feelings of anger, sadness, and shame that she thought she'd gotten over long ago. Each song and brushstroke elicited a more visceral response than the last. It had been almost two years. It baffled her how this could feel so fresh after so long. After so many sexcapades and countless women who'd offered a fleeting feeling of connection.

Shouldn't that be enough? All of that should've taken care of the heartbreak, no? It felt like it in the moment, so why doesn't it now?

Once she emerged from the shower, she was nowhere to be found in the after-party. In her place, Gabby stepped in and schmoozed with the buyers, promising that Viv would appear shortly.

Ryan, sensing that something was off from watching Viv's body language backstage after the show, looked at her watch and knew too much time had passed. She wandered through the gallery across the arena and found Viv in the studio, sitting at her desk, staring blankly at her computer that showed nothing but a blank browser.

"Vivi?" She softly ran her hand across the back of Viv's shoulders. "What are you doing over here? Everyone's waiting for you. Here, I brought your go-go juice for you," she said, extending the glass in Viv's direction.

Viv responded, her head and gaze unmoved, "I don't want a drink right now."

Ryan had never seen Viv refuse a drink. She knew whatever was on her mind was serious. She pulled up a stool and placed her hand on Viv's knee, rubbing it lightly with her thumb. "What's going on?"

"I can't do this, Ry," Viv replied barely above a whisper. Her eyes glistened with tears as her emotions welled up.

Ryan, trying to understand, asked, "Do what? The after-party? So don't. You're the boss."

"Not the party. Not the schmoozing. Not the shows." She rubbed her hand across her forehead as she said, "I can't do *this*. This fake thing we've been doing for months now."

Belle's comments about Ryan hadn't been lost on Viv. She had trapped Ryan in another world of lies. A world where she couldn't live one hundred percent in her truth. One where she had limited decision-making power. She didn't deserve that.

Ryan leaned over to make eye contact and tried to be reassuring. "Vivi, I told you already. It doesn't bother me."

"But you're not telling me what *does* bother you!" Viv blurted out. "What you care about. What you want. Don't get me wrong, Ry, I…I love you…but you're always so fucking selfless, *especially* when it comes to me, but you shouldn't be. You deserve to be happy, to live your life on your terms."

Shut up before you make things worse.

"I'm not saying that I'm not happy we reconnected, because I am. But this charade can't continue." Viv couldn't bring herself to look in Ryan's direction. She slumped down in her chair in a huff and stared at her hands.

This isn't even a real breakup. So why does it feel like one?

Ryan was taken aback by Viv's statement, unsure of how to respond. "I…I don't know what to say."

"There's nothing to say. It's not your fault. It's mine for agreeing to it in the first place. I'll work out details with Gabby on how to untangle this. I need to go." Viv scooted her chair back and motioned for Zo to take her home before Gabby noticed.

***

Viv didn't go home. A block or so after leaving the studio, she instructed Zo to take her to see Sylvie. She sat silently in the back for the entire drive, chain-smoking cigarettes as her mind raced. They arrived at TOP just before 10:00 p.m.

Every table was full, as it usually was at that hour. Regulars immediately noticed Viv, less for who she was and more for the fact that this was not one of the usual nights she came in. Viv, still in a trance, glided past their watchful eyes and gently knocked on the door of Sylvie's office.

"Come in!" she yelled from behind the door. She was stunned to see Viv walk in. "Hey, bro! What are you doing here? Wasn't your show tonight?"

"Yeah, yeah, it was." Viv sat in the extra chair in the office. Visibly shaken, she clasped her hands together on the desk, careful to not get any residual paint anywhere. She stared pensively at Sylvie. "I had to bail on the party. I need to talk to you."

Sylvie sat up straight. "Yeah, man. What's going on?"

"I think it's time for Ryan and me to 'break up,'" Viv said using air quotes.

Sylvie's face scrunched up upon hearing those words. "But, dude, why? Everything's going great. Why ruin a good thing? You're rolling in cash again. The media loves you. You're having fun together, no doubt. You're happy. She's happy."

"Is she?" Viv interjected, hitting the table with her hand, "Really? Is she? Ry's always been easy going, but enough's enough. She deserves to be *happy*."

Sylvie threw it right back. "How do you know she's not?"

"I don't know," Viv quickly retorted.

"Did you ask her explicitly?" Sylvie pressed on.

"No." She'd come looking for advice and an empathetic ear, but Viv suddenly felt as if she were in an interrogation.

Their rapid-fire conversation continued. "Did she hint that she wasn't?"

"No."

"Then HOW do you know?" Sylvie's voice rose as she leaned towards Viv.

Viv's voice and body language mimicked Sylvie's. "How do YOU?"

"Because she fucking bought *Geraldine* and *Henri*!" Sylvie's hand slammed against her desk. Her eyes widened as she mouthed, "Fuck," instantly realizing she'd broken Ryan's confidence.

Viv leaned back in her chair with a wide-eyed, confused look on her face. "What?"

"She bought *Geraldine* and *Henri*," Sylvie said softer, regaining her composure. "The anonymous buyer. That was her."

Viv shook her head in disbelief. "How can you be so sure?" Her voice cracked as she spoke.

Sylvie leaned against her desk and scratched her forehead as she spoke, "Listen, I tried *every* day to get her to come to the funeral, but she wouldn't budge. She wanted to come, but after what happened at Jack's funeral, she was convinced that her being there in person would only make things worse. I finally got her to let me FaceTime her in for the tribute show. After she saw you break down, she texted me for the rest of the night to be the highest bidder for both paintings. As strongly as she felt that her absence was for the best, she felt even stronger that you should be the only one to own and decide the fate of those canvases."

Viv was trying to make sense of this information. "Okay, but then...where'd she get that kind of money?"

Sylvie continued to fill in the gaps, "Jack didn't have a will before he died. If he did, I'm sure he wouldn't have given a dime to Ryan. But because he didn't, inheritance laws in New York state that his estate goes to his remaining descendant, which is Ry. She wanted no connection with Todd ever again, so my uncle negotiated that she keep the entirety of the estate in exchange for no alimony payments.

"Once the agreement was done, she had more than enough to provide a decent life for a little over a decade. About fifteen, maybe twenty years, if she skimped on some things. Buying those paintings would cut that window in half, more than, if I remember correctly. I asked her if she was sure, over and over, but she was adamant about it. She said to beat each new high bid by thirty percent to quickly knock out the competition, including the final bids, just before the window closed, so she wouldn't be blindsided."

Viv sat in complete silence, shell-shocked. Very few things rendered her speechless, but this did. Simultaneously, the lingering guilt she felt about having Ryan trapped in a fake relationship, while Viv got to freely live her life, cut even deeper.

Why would she do that?

Sylvie continued, "You two are *ob-freaking-sessed* with each other. Always have been. Like, to unhealthy levels when you're out of sync. You always talk about her. She always talks about you. You both suck at communication though. You can't say anything that you feel will take away from this walking billboard brand that Gabby makes you believe you have to be. And she can't speak up for herself if she's not in the driver's seat or there's a chance of rejection. You guys need, like, couples counseling or some shit."

"Yeah, because that totally saved your marriage, right?" Viv said sarcastically.

"No, it didn't, asshole, but it helped me see unhealthy patterns," Sylvie continued. "You still love her, and she clearly still loves you. I know it. Gabby knows it. Zo knows it. The only person that doesn't know it, or maybe just doesn't believe it, is you. She'd obviously move heaven and earth for you, and vice versa. Christ, dude, just fucking help me understand what the fuck is going on with you because this is confusing as shit. And I know you better than anyone."

"Sylv, this is just…a lot to process. I can't even… I don't think… I don't know." Viv, waving her hands in front of her, was mentally and physically drained.

Sylvie grabbed her hand empathetically and lowered her tone as she said, "Hey. I got you. No matter what. Just sleep on it at least, okay?"

Viv nodded before rising from her seat. "I will. I gotta go."

***

The next morning it was Viv, not Gabby, texting at an unreasonable hour.

Viv: We need to talk.

Viv: Can you get here by 7?

Gabby arrived at Viv's condo shortly after seven, where she met Viv standing at the elevator door and extending her hand with a coffee. "Jesus, you're up early, and you're giving me coffee. This must be serious."

"It is. I need you to listen. Really listen and know that I'm not taking no for an answer," Viv said matter-of-factly as she sat on the coffee table opposite the couch, where Gabby sat attentively waiting to hear what was on her client's mind.

Gabby attempted to sway Viv out of fabricating a breakup, as Viv had expected, because of the amount of press the series was getting and how much momentum they'd have after Ryan's show. This wasn't Gabby's first rodeo with Viv wanting to put her foot down. She appreciated that Viv talked a big game, but in the end, she knew she could spin any hesitation into a yes.

She patiently waited until Viv finished making her case. "Okay. I heard you. And what happens if I don't approve of this plan?"

"You're fired, and you can get the fuck out of my house," Viv said flatly before rising and walking towards the window.

Gabby jumped up. "Viv! Hey, hey now. Your mom hired me to do what's best for you. Remember?"

Viv's head snapped around. "She hired you to do what's best for my career. *Not* my personal life! We're not zeros and ones in a spreadsheet. Or x's and o's in a playbook. We're fucking human beings. Business in, business out, remember?" Viv was undeterred. At some point, they had to jump off this runaway train, and that time was now.

Gabby reluctantly agreed and sat back down to hammer out the details. They agreed that the split wouldn't occur until a few weeks after Ryan's show, to give it and her the attention and praise she deserved. The mechanics of what would cause the split weren't yet worked out, but they agreed that Ryan's image was to remain untarnished. They'd release a joint statement stating either that they'd agreed on being creative partners, rather than lovers, or that Viv would take the blame as she falsely had before.

Ryan's space in the studio would be hers permanently, or for as long as she liked. If she preferred to work elsewhere, they'd scout the best space on the market and pay for it for a year. Finally, their public engagements would be minimal after the fashion show.

"Anything else?" Gabby asked, tugging at her shirttails.

"No. You can go now. I'll be in later." Viv sipped on her drink while gesturing with her eyes towards the elevator.

Gabby left Viv to her thoughts after shaking hands on the terms discussed. As she walked herself to the elevator, she stopped at the picture of Geraldine and Henri. "You know," she said with an ironic smirk, turning her head towards Viv, "they'd be so proud of you right now."

Chapter 22

Shake Shack

Viv skipped going into the studio for the rest of the day. It had been a heavy twelve hours. She needed space away from everything and everyone to breathe. Less than a week ago, everything was fine, but suddenly it all seemed to be falling apart at once. If she was being honest with herself, the arrangement between her and Ryan had felt wrong from the day that Ryan explained the truth about their breakup.

It was easy for the casual outsider to believe that Viv was a self-indulgent human and borderline narcissistic. She grew up as an only child with parents who made her the center of their universe. In her professional life, as a walking brand, she was also the center of the universe. She was the main event. Aside from Alana, in her adult life, she'd never made space for anyone else's feelings or opinions that weren't those of her parents. She never had to.

Gabby was the only person who could make her into a marionette for the sake of her career; she managed to pull her strings no matter how hard Viv resisted. Though, up to now, it had never mattered that much to Viv because she had been the only one affected. She wasn't oblivious to the fact that from the start of this charade, both Ryan's life and hers would be impacted. But at that time, she resented Ryan so much that Ryan's feelings would've held no weight, even if she'd voiced them.

All of that had changed now. She knew that the end of their relationship in college had been out of Ryan's hands. And thanks to Sylvie, she also knew that Ryan sacrificed her own financial security to buy *Geraldine* and *Henri*, thereby giving Viv the greatest gift she had ever received. Drunk or sober, Viv historically had never been great at processing her feelings, but today felt especially insurmountable.

She threw on a black hoodie and gray sweats, took a bottle of pinot grigio out of the refrigerator and her lawn chair out of the junk closet, and grabbed her car keys. She drove out to the cemetery to sit with her parents. It was a foggy day, as it usually is in Colma. Mist was present in the air and brushed against Viv's face as she exited her car. She fumbled getting her chair situated while she cradled the wine underneath her right arm. Once she managed to uncork the wine and get settled in the chair, she slouched down, lit a cigarette, and took several sips of pinot.

Mom. Dad. I wish you were here. I don't know what I'm doing anymore. What's right? What's fair? What do I even want anymore?

Paired with her deep confusion was equal surprise to find herself here, back in this same position, feeling the weight and heartache of her parents' death, the heartlessness of Alana, and the emptiness she felt by the absence of Ryan at the funeral proceedings. This time, she felt additional pain from the presence of Ryan and her newly discovered generosity, repressed feelings about how Alana handled their breakup, and the perpetual loss of her parents as sounding boards. She could only imagine what they would say to her now. She tried briefly before stopping herself as she wasn't confident that she'd just make up what she wanted to hear.

The different catalysts for the pain she felt inside were mixing together and being compounded by each other, as they had two years ago. Fake relationship or not, Ryan was everything Alana wasn't—kind, thoughtful, patient, genuine. She never had an ulterior motive. There wasn't a vengeful bone in her body. She wondered if part of her attraction to a mate who was the polar opposite was because she felt she didn't deserve the type of love that Ryan gave her.

Alana said it herself, *"How can anyone love that?"*

Maybe Sylvie was right in saying that the love her parents had for each other was a fluke. That lightning couldn't strike twice. That she couldn't be sure it was true love at such a young age; perhaps it was just a matter of coincidence and circumstance.

The night grounds manager, Nick, arrived for his shift, recognized Viv, and stopped his car on his way to the office. "Ms. Roche?" he yelled out with concerned eyes.

"Just a short visit today, Nick! I promise!" she yelled back as she waved him off with the bottle of wine in her hand.

He nodded and continued on to the office as Viv nestled back into her thoughts.

She returned home a few hours later and kept her mind busy, but focused. She sat on her loveseat while she read the reviews for each show in the series that Gabby had emailed her, as well as the press for Ryan's show.

Over several weeks, the buzz for the finale had grown such that the studio wasn't big enough. Gabby arranged for the show to take place at the Julia Morgan Ballroom. Despite her quest for peace, all evening her phone lit up with texts and DMs from past flings and flames attempting to lure her out for a romp or two. What would usually entice her, and cause her to have Zo set up her usual accommodations, felt like a thousand little cuts to her heart.

She settled in front of her TV, which was set just below *Geraldine* and leaned back on her oversized sectional on the opposite wall beneath *Henri*. She took long, slow drags from a fresh cigarette while she turned on *Footloose*. She remembered the conversation with Ryan back in college, when she "sort of came out," as she would describe it. In the moment, she was equally confused by why it was such a big deal, wanting to comfort her and wanting to share her true feelings, but fearing it would appear selfish. She remembered how agonizing it was coaching Ryan on how to flirt and watching her go off with other women. She wondered if Ryan felt the same.

I mean, she did say she wanted to come out to me and share her true emotions that night, but was afraid that I'd reject her.

Viv noodled on history repeating itself. *Is that why she came back?* She rubbed her eyes with her palms, nestled under a blanket, and eventually fell asleep.

***

When Viv returned to the studio the next morning, she found Ryan buzzing around between the models for the show, pinning and taking notes for the adjustments that needed to be made. To Viv's surprise, when Ryan noticed her, she was as chipper as ever.

"Vivi, good you're here. I'm just about done with the models. Can you change into your clothes, so we can check the fit?"

Ryan had designed an elegant garment for Viv to wear. The base was ivory. The top was a fairly simple scoop neck with cutoff sleeves, a cape-like jacket sewn into the neckline of the shirt, and the strands of the jacket draping the arms, so it flowed when Viv walked. Sewn on the seams at the base of the shirt were small lavender strips of fabric that ran up and over the neckline before extending beyond the cape. The pants were a simple high-waisted style with chic vertical rips along the front pleats and the side seams to evoke the ethereal nature of Viv's work.

Once in the ensemble, Viv tried to use their working session to address their last conversation. "Hey, Ry. About the other night. Can we—"

Ryan didn't look up from her work. "Gabby already briefed me. She's coming up with the postshow plan for this whole *thing* to end."

Viv was a bit taken aback by her curtness. "Yeah, but I unilaterally made that decision. It affects both of us, so you should have an opinion too. I'm trying to make space for you to share that."

Ryan remained unbothered. "Nope. It all sounds good to me. No input. Now, stop moving before I prick you."

"Come on, Ry. You have to have an op—"

"VIV! Like I said. It's fine. I'm fine. I'm fine with it."

"Y-You never call me Viv."

"That's your name, isn't it?" Ryan snapped before shaking her head while letting out a deep breath. "We don't need to keep complicating things. Let's just keep having fun while we can. We'll do whatever Gabby comes up with, and we'll go on with our lives. Speaking of, you're good to go. You can change out of this, so I can get back to work," she said, shooing Viv away with her hands, before rising from her stool, grabbing her notebook, and scribbling furiously for a few minutes. She scratched out a few large areas and continued her impassioned writing. Viv had changed and returned to the studio by the time she was done.

"Gabby! Set list for the show," Ryan said, handing it over as Gabby approached with an outstretched arm.

Gabby scanned the list. "Good shit, kid. We've got you covered."

"Set list?" Viv asked warily.

"Vivi, I can't do a show about your work without adding the signature element, storytelling," Ryan replied.

"Can I see it?"

Ryan played coy, almost flirtatious, with a smile on her face. "Absolutely not. Got to leave something to the imagination."

Viv looked at Gabby, who held her hands up. "Don't look at me. Right now, I'm her manager too. She's the boss," she said before walking away.

***

In the days that followed, Ryan was her usual jovial and bubbly self. Viv was cautiously comfortable, but she could no longer get a read on Ryan. *Is she mad, but playing the part? Does she really not care? Will ending the charade turn out to be a massive disaster? Will she pull an Alana and drag my name through the mud?* These thoughts haunted Viv day and night. She elected to focus her attention on the ideas she had for shows once the series and breakup was complete.

***

The day of the show, Larry was scheduled to drop off Ryan at Viv's garage, where Zo would take them both to the venue for preshow photos and schmoozing. Instead, Ryan showed up, and Zo told her that when he arrived, he went upstairs to check, but Viv wasn't there. She tried calling, but it went straight to voice mail. Knowing that Viv wouldn't ghost her big show, Ryan accurately guessed that Viv was in the studio working.

"Vivi! What are you doing here? You were supposed to be ready by now. You left your outfit at your place. Here!" she said, extending her arm out.

Viv pulled off her headphones. "Ugh, I'm sorry, Ry. I lost track of time without the usual noise, since everyone is at a different venue on show day. I'm just finishing up oooone email to a vennnndoooor annnd...done."

"Okay, hurry. Take a quick shower and change so we're not late. Gabby's been blowing up my phone all day. Is this every day for you?" Ryan asked.

"Yep. Welcome to my hell. I'll be ready in ten," Viv said, grabbing the clothes from Ryan.

As she walked hurriedly towards the bathroom, Ryan yelled out, "Hey, Vivi! You forgot to send the email. Do you want me to do it?"

"Yes, please!" Viv responded from inside the bathroom. The water flowing from the shower could faintly be heard.

Ryan went to send it, but accidentally clicked where the cursor was hovering and closed the email.

Damn it. Might as well sit down and do this properly while I wait.

As Ryan's eyes moved to the draft folder, she noticed that there were 128 draft emails saved. She originally meant to simply open the email, send it, and close Viv's laptop. Instead, she was shaken by what she saw. Every draft email started with "Dear Ryan, I thought about you today." She opened a few to read them.

December 21, 2007: I heard you got married. I couldn't bring myself to go. Did you get my gift?

May 24, 2007: I found your beanie when I packed up the apartment with my parents. Remember it? You said it was your bat signal for being gay? It still smells faintly like you.

September 1, 2010: Do you remember when you went to the Diesel store after your first show and you spent your money on that dress that looked like a trash bag? God, I hated that dress…

February 12, 2008: I tried explaining to a bartender about that crazy drink we had once, the Pineapple of Hospitality one. The one that came on fire? They didn't get it.

October 11, 2010: I heard that new song by Sara Bareilles. King of Anything. I'm sure you're feeling vindicated by her success since you called it YEARS ago.

March 16, 2008: I spent so many hours hunting down the buyers from your first show. I bought one of each design with the checks from my first official art show. I'm not sure why really. Maybe it makes me feel closer to you. Maybe one day you'd want them.

March 30, 2014: It's 2:37 in the morning. All I can think about are your pinky caresses when you wanted to have sex.

December 4, 2012: I watched the sunset at the Ladies Pavilion in Central Park. This used to be our spot when we wanted to escape from the world together.

November 11, 2018: Remember when we froze on that balcony in Philly? You told me that outside of fashion you felt invisible. It broke my heart then and it still does.

February 7, 2011: I remember insisting that we date properly even though we'd already had sex and knew everything about each other. My anxiety spiked when you were late...23 minutes late to be exact...I thought you stood me up but it was just the stupid 6 Train breaking down again.

April 17, 2015: Today is my dad's birthday. I still remember how happy you were when he took you on that horse buggy ride outside Radio City Music Hall. It was our tradition, but you deserved a Father-Daughter moment too.

July 14, 2016: This show I'm working on is killing me. I'm pulling all-nighters again but without your energy it feels more lonely. There were so many nights you worked longer than me. I miss feeling you get in bed so I could give you one of my 'lullaby massages' you loved so much with my 'magic hands' as you called them.

June 5, 2009: I went parasailing today. You never liked parasailing. You always wanted to be on a hot air balloon.

January 2, 2011: They closed that bar we went to a couple times. The one where we ordered one drink just so we could make out while our friends partied. You left her a 300% tip. I still don't think she liked us because *she charged us $11 each for an Irish Car Bomb. We called them Ferrari Bombs after that night. Fuck that place.*

August 8, 2013: You were so cute when we first started dating when it came to PDA. Stolen kisses at the flagpole, in the corners of subway stations, waiting for our Shake Shack order, at the fruit stands at the Farmer's Markets.

Ryan read countless entries from over the past twelve years; Viv had written emails to her, but never sent them. All full of memories, questions, stray observations. Each one ended the same.

I hope you're happy. I still love you. Vivi

Ryan sat back in Viv's chair in disbelief, her tongue running back and forth along the inside of her lip.

When Viv emerged from the bathroom, she had her game face on, ready to own the night. Her smile broke when she saw Ryan's face. "What's wrong?"

"Vivi"—she didn't turn to make eye contact—"what the fuck?"

"What? What did I do?"

Ryan gestured at the laptop.

Viv was speechless when she saw what was on the screen. There was no rebuttal that would diffuse the situation. "Ry, listen...I...uh—"

"You what?" Ryan's top had suddenly blown. She stood up and walked past Viv a few steps before turning around, her voice rising with each word as she said, "You resent me. Treat me like dog shit because of how you *thought* our breakup happened. You fight this fake relationship and act like I'm a stranger. You do a show saying 'fuck you' to your ex-fiancée, only to turn around and say you want to break up when the WHOLE FUCKING TIME you've been writing little love notes since college?"

Viv tried reaching out to touch Ryan's arm softly. "Ry, no… no… Listen. I just—"

Ryan pulled away and shook her head, tears forming in her eyes, "No! Fuck you! It doesn't make sense. Tell me how this makes sense to you!"

"Ry, I…" Viv sighed, unable to find her words. She was frozen like a statue. Her body felt as if every hair were standing on end.

"Tell me!" Ryan exclaimed, tears rolling down her face.

Viv's façade snapped. "What do you want me to say? Huh? That I missed you? That I never got over you? That I've compared every single woman that I've ever encountered to you? That you were right about my art? That I used the auction idea from your show for my shows because it made me feel close to you? That there's not a single day that's gone by that I don't think of you? That I use my art as a crutch for not actually dealing with shit and my emotions? That I've drunkenly made my way through the last decade plus, just so I can push those thoughts away? That when my parents died, you were the one person I wanted to call? The one I wanted there while I cried? That the only person that I ever truly loved not showing up on the worst day of my life broke my psyche beyond belief? That you appearing at the end of my show felt like you just came to twist that knife in my heart? That these past few months have been the happiest that I've been since my parents died? That I understand now why we ended and that I want so badly to trust you and open up and tell you that I was wrong? That I don't want this to end? That I want it to be real, but I'm scared to death of you breaking my heart again? Is that what you want? Is that what you want to hear? Is that what you wanted to fucking hear, Ryan?" Viv had exhausted herself.

A lump had grown in Ryan's throat with every word Viv said. "Well…yeah! That would've been great to hear…like FOREVER ago!" Ryan exclaimed with her eyes wide-open and matching Viv's display of emotion.

They stood in silence, Ryan staring at Viv, who in turn held her head lowered as she stared at her feet. Both were breathing deeply, their hearts racing from the heated exchange.

Ryan took a step towards Viv, softly grabbing her left hand with her right. "Did you really buy one of each item from my first collection?"

Viv looked up to meet Ryan's gaze and took her own step forward, further closing the gap between them and grabbing Ryan's left hand with her right. "Did you really buy *Geraldine* and *Henri*?"

Ryan sucked air through her teeth, looked at the ground, and whispered, "Fucking Sylvie."

Viv removed her hands and gently placed them on Ryan's face, tilting Ryan's head to meet her eyes. She leaned her forehead against Ryan's and felt their heavy breaths intertwine.

Ryan moved slightly to place a kiss softly on Viv's left cheek. "I missed you," she whispered. She felt Viv smiling at her comment and lingered, pressed cheek to cheek while she felt Viv's desire growing.

Viv moved back slightly to meet Ryan's lips with hers. Clumsily at first. She jumped back slightly at the heat ignited within her once their lips touched.

Ryan, unbeknownst of that, jumped back as well. "Did you feel it too?" she asked.

Viv nodded before moving closer to kiss her again. This time more confidently. The world around them melted away. Ryan's lips were softer than she remembered. Ryan grabbed her by the hips so their bodies could meet, squeezing Viv's lower back tightly while their lips and tongues continued to explore each other. The years of pain, self-doubt, and longing no longer existed. They exchanged several deep pants between them, making contact with each other before Ryan went for another kiss.

A few seconds later, Viv pulled away.

Ryan was thrown off. "Vivi, what's happening? Did I do something wrong."

"No, no you didn't. It's me," she replied, choking on her words as she fought back tears. "I just can't. I'm so sorry, Ry. I want to, but I can't."

Ryan grabbed Viv's hand, stroking the back of it with her thumb. "Vivi, I understand. We can take it slow. We don't have to get married tomorrow. Can't we both acknowledge that we're still in love with each other? Can't we take this leap of faith together? Fear and all?"

Viv pulled her hand away. "I-I...I can't. I'm sorry." Viv wiped her tears away as she walked towards the exit, where Zo had patiently been waiting outside.

Ryan, completely dejected, watched her walk out of the studio. She wiped the tears out of her eyes before finding her resolve and heading towards the door as well.

Get it together, Ry. There's a show to do.

Chapter 23

Footloose

Viv settled into her seat in the front row. She'd spent the past hour dodging questions about what those in attendance could expect from the final show in the series. The name, *Ryan's Love*, didn't give any clues to the subject matter. When asked for comments in the weeks prior to the show, Ryan's response never wavered. "That's what you're all going to show up for and find out, isn't it?"

Sylvie showed up a few minutes before showtime. "Hey, dude, sorry I'm late. Traffic was crazy coming off the bridge. I went backstage to wish Ry luck. She looks *good*. Focused as hell. I brought you a beer."

Viv, half hearing her, half spaced-out, had a delayed reaction to the bottle in front of her face. "Hmmm? Oh, thanks, bro. Glad you're here."

"Cheers. To Ry!" Sylvie grinned as she tapped their bottles together.

Viv took a deep breath, holding the bottle with both hands before lifting it in cheers to the air. "Yeah…to Ry."

"You okay?"

"Never better."

"You're lying." Sylvie knew better than to believe curt Viv.

"You know me," Viv said dryly, sipping on her beer. "Can we do this after the show? Tonight's not about me."

Sylvie put her hands up, signaling she was backing off. They sat silently staring across to the photographers on the other side of the runway. Spectators were surprised to see a reimagined arena when they arrived. In its place was a white runway that ran two-thirds the length of the room. White chairs flanked either side of the runway, and two screens hung on either side of the wall where the models would emerge from backstage.

Gabby arrived at her seat just behind Viv before the show began. "This is gonna be good, kid. Press is eating this up. We should've done a series years ago," she said, shaking Viv's shoulder.

Viv took a deep breath and tried to let go of what happened at the studio only hours ago. "Never again, Gab."

The lights went down, signaling the show was about to begin. Over the PA system, a voice could be heard saying, "Esteemed attendees, members of the media, and VIPs, for your consideration, we present to you *Ryan's Love: The Roche Collection*."

The show began up-tempo. Within seconds of Marvin Gaye and Tammi Terrell's "Ain't No Mountain High Enough" coming through the speakers, two models appeared from backstage as Viv's work was projected against the wall on either side of the runway. Ryan chose to open with *Geraldine* and *Henri*, as they were the most recognizable of Viv's portfolio. The models chosen closely resembled their subject matter in appearance, and the robes draped them perfectly. They posed and twirled with the joy the song called for, performing the banter in the lyrics, chasing playfully after each other, and dancing in unison.

As the chorus started, a third model, about twelve, resembling Viv at that age, appeared in a black robe of similar styling to that of the original pieces. The adult models met her at the rear of the runway, and the three of them ran hand in hand up the runway, the adults lifting the child and swinging her back and forth as she laughed.

The addition of the third model to the performance was a complete surprise to Viv, who had neither been informed nor ever seen her during numerous rehearsals. She shared a look with Sylvie before sitting up intently, her elbows resting squarely on her knees, and her chin resting on her fists.

The show continued the old-school feeling with the Temptations' "Ain't Too Proud to Beg," before shifting to current pop music with Rihanna's "We Found Love." Each piece was different from the last, mirroring the eclectic nature of Viv's work. "We Found Love" was a tattered, trumpet-styled wedding dress; whereas, for Lady Gaga's "Stupid Love," the models wore designs that made reference to Japanese B-boys, and for Katy Perry's "Unconditionally," the model donned a perfectly tailored body suit with a dramatically flared train made out of army camouflage and green fatigue boots.

The crowd was captivated by Ryan's range and was on the edge of their seats as each model made their exit for the next model to appear.

Viv was on the edge of her seat as well, but for a different reason. Ryan's design prowess was not new to her. She was, however, taken by the set list that was chosen. She pondered if Ryan was actually speaking to her, or if that was just a convenient lie she was telling herself. The show became more pointed as Alicia Keys's "No One," Pink and Nate Ruess's "Just Give Me a Reason," and Lauryn Hill's "Ex-Factor," preceded the dramatic Toni Braxton's "Un-Break My Heart."

Before the final look was set to hit the runway, images from *Immersive Love* were projected as the soothing chords of Al Green's "Let's Stay Together" began to play. The final look was a full-length ballroom gown made up of hundreds, if not thousands, of pieces of fabrics sewn together using the same hues of blues and lavender. The garment was chaotically elegant, with different types of fabrics—Lycra, denim, chiffon, tulle—giving way to one another. As busy as it was when you zoomed into the details, it was undeniably a standout look that just worked effortlessly.

Ryan had been peeking from her spot backstage, watching both the models' and the crowd's reactions, but her main focus was on Viv. She knew that music spoke to Viv in a way that words or actions never could. As the models took their final walks, she saw Viv swaying happily back and forth to the lyrics.

Ryan took to the stage holding a microphone and received a standing ovation from the crowd. She beamed as she waited for the applause to settle before she spoke. "Good evening, everyone! Thank you, thank you! This night has been more than I could have ever hoped for. I do want to acknowledge the inspiration for all of the looks you've seen tonight—the fabulous Vivienne Roche!"

The spotlight found Viv, who stood briefly and waved.

As the applause ended, Ryan continued, "Over the course of the *Love Series*, you've been seeing pieces of what makes Vivi tick. This is new to all of you, but I've known *this* Viv since I stole her coffee when we were eighteen. Believe me, she won't let me forget it." Laughter rang out across the room. "She's many things and has many talents. One in particular…is lying."

Gabby's voice sprang into Viv's ear, "Viv, you've g—"

"Shut. Up. Gabby," Viv said through gritted teeth. She didn't turn her head; her eyes were locked on Ryan, while everyone else's were locked on Viv.

"Viv's been lying to all of you. We did an interview the morning after *Immersive Love*. When asked why we broke up, she said she cheated on me. That's not true. The love that Vivi showered me with was the greatest love I've ever felt. The kind where someone sees you, all of you, the brilliant parts and the messy bits. How could anyone not love that?" She paused and took a deep breath in front of a crowd hanging on her every word. "I fucked up. I broke her heart, not the other way around. A lot was out of my control, but I could've done something. *Anything*. At least tried. But I didn't."

She turned to face Viv, locking eyes. "I wasn't brave enough to truly love myself, let alone to tell her. Vivi, I love you more than anything in this world, and I promise you that I will never break your heart again. I know you're scared. I'm scared too. Please don't give up on us."

In a room full of hundreds, they only saw each other. Viv rose and extended her hand. Ryan placed the microphone down on the runway and walked in Viv's direction. Once she was close enough, Viv grabbed her by her lower back, spun a quarter turn as she picked Ryan up, and lowered her to the floor.

Ryan draped her arms around Viv's neck and whispered, "I'm so in love with you it hurts. Can you stop lying to yourself for once?"

Viv placed both arms around Ryan's waist, pulled her closer, and flashed a small smile. "I love you too."

As they kissed, the cacophony of camera flashes was almost blinding. They saw nothing and felt nothing but each other. Sparks ran from head to toe for Viv, jolting through Ryan. Just past them, Gabby could be seen beaming and rapidly sending off texts to press contacts.

During the after-party, they didn't leave each other's side. Viv stood patiently in the distance while Ryan did her interviews, with Viv enjoying both Ryan's success and the ability to be a fan instead of the main event for once. When the interviews concluded, they behaved like grade-schoolers, running towards each other. The remainder of the after-party was a blur for both of them. The countless faces and photo ops were replaced by stolen arm caresses and heated stares.

About an hour before the end of the schmoozing, there was a brief moment that they weren't swamped with people. Viv felt Ryan's pinky run up her arm and trace down her back. They shared a brief look before Viv swung her head around to spot Zo and signal that it was time to go. They quickly turned and ran for the door, hand in hand, as if they had dined and dashed.

While Zo drove, their hands explored what they could in his presence. Ryan licked and bit behind Viv's ear before she nibbled on her earlobe, and her tongue explored every crevice. Ryan's hot breath in Viv's ear made Viv let out a deep sigh. She responded by placing her hand under Ryan's dress and running it up her thigh before squeezing her ass. As she did, her pinky grazed Ryan's pussy that had soaked her underwear hours before.

Ryan's body lunged forward towards Viv in response as Ryan let out a small moan. "Mmmhhhmmph," she bit her lip, trying to control herself. They could not reach their destination soon enough.

Once inside, Viv put her hands around Ryan's neck and jumped up, wrapping her legs around her waist. Ryan cupped her ass with her hands and spun to press Viv's back against the door they'd just closed. Ryan licked up and around Viv's neck, sucking and even biting at certain moments. Viv wrapped her legs tighter to pull Ryan in closer as her body shook. She whispered in Ryan's ear, "Fuck me."

Ryan responded with a passionate kiss, their tongues dancing. "Yes, ma'am." She clumsily carried Viv to the bed, bumping into the doorframe before charting the right path. They shared a laugh as Ryan laid Viv down gently.

Viv bent her legs, running her left foot up her right calf, arms stretched out above her. She had a moment of self-doubt. She'd wanted Ryan back for so long, and now she froze at the thought of no longer being able to meet Ryan's desires.

Ryan noticed the look in Viv's eyes and sat up. "Nervous?"

Viv nodded.

Ryan scooted to the edge of the bed and kissed Viv's pussy through her pants, running her tongue along the length of it.

The fabric was thin, and Viv could feel the warmth and wetness of Ryan's tongue. She let out a deep moan, trying to catch her breath.

"How about now?" Ryan asked.

Viv shook her head no.

"Good." Ryan proceeded to pull Viv's pants off, followed by her own. They took turns removing each other's clothing until they were standing naked in front of each other.

"You're so beautiful." Viv took in the beauty that was Ryan's body, before gently pushing her back on the bed, crawling on top of her in the process. Their bodies pressed firmly against each other. "Do you think we can switch?" Viv asked between kisses.

Ryan nodded before lying on the other side of the bed.

Viv was normally a ravenous lover when she was as horny as she was now, but she wanted to savor as much of the moment as she could. She traced circles around Ryan's nipples, biting them gently until Ryan let out a loud moan, her body arching in the air in response. Viv made her way between Ryan's legs and wasted no time, strongly licking from the bottom of her pussy up to her clit. Ryan's body convulsed under her touch as she let out another loud moan. Viv shook her head with a sly grin on her face. "Fuck...you're so fucking wet."

"Come here," Ryan replied, summoning Viv with her finger. "I want to feel how wet you are." Viv crawled back over her body until she was close enough for Ryan to run three fingers over her dripping pussy. Being the sly tease that she was, Ryan briefly slipped her middle finger inside Viv's eager opening.

Viv leaned over Ryan in response, with her arms fully extended, trying to keep her balance. She bent her arms slightly to get close enough for another kiss. The desperation between them was at its peak. Viv pushed herself back up onto her knees and placed one knee between Ryan's legs and the other on the outside of her right hip. She grabbed on to Ryan's left leg for support. "Let me know when it's good for you?"

Ryan nodded as Viv lowered herself down for their clits to meet each other. Viv changed her position a few times before Ryan's hands gripped the sheets. "Uuuuunnf, right there, right there, right there!"

Viv rammed her body against Ryan's. Their pussies slid over each other rhythmically; each time their clits touched, they both let out load moans. Viv's breath became labored as her thrusts quickened and she applied more pressure. Ryan's back arched off the bed as she responded to the pleasure. The next instant that their clits connected, Viv shortened her stroke, placing all of her energy in one spot.

With both their nerve endings overstimulated, Viv threw her head back as she came, several waves crashing across her.

Ryan grabbed Viv's forearm as she came in unison, her body pressing against Viv, increasing the pleasure. "Fuck, fuck, fuck, fuck, fuuuuuck." She collapsed back on the bed.

Viv lowered her leg and laid her sweaty body on Ryan's. They exchanged deep, passionate kisses. Viv paused briefly to stare at Ryan, stroking the scar on her forehead softly. "I love you."

"I love you too," Ryan said as she pulled Viv in for another kiss.

***

The next morning, they lay in each other's arms, legs intertwined. The sun streamed through the floor-to-ceiling windows of Viv's bedroom and the skylights unique to the penthouse units. They'd barely slept all night, exploring each other over and over again.

Viv kissed Ryan's shoulder and nuzzled her neck with her face before they exchanged gentle, sleepy kisses.

Viv's phone began buzzing incessantly. "Mmmmmmmmm." Viv rubbed her eyes as she grabbed her phone and saw the texts from Gabby that continued to stream in.

Ryan traced Viv's stomach with her fingers. "Work?"

"Yeah." Viv let out a deep sigh.

"Want me to go?" Ryan wrapped her legs tighter around Viv.

Viv looked back at her phone, turned it off, and threw it across the room. She pulled Ryan in close for another kiss. "No," she whispered, "I want you to stay."

Acknowledgments

One of the scariest things for a creative of any medium is to share their creation with the world for consumption and opinion. Writing is the most personal thing I can do. It's always there, waiting for me to come back to it when I'm ready to pick it back up. As a child, I excelled in explaining my thoughts and opinions. Expressing my feelings, however, was where I struggled mightily. Thankfully, I was introduced to creative writing in elementary school at Dr. George Washington Carver Elementary in San Francisco, and it felt as if a dam had burst. I found out I was blessed with a gift, and thereafter, within the written form of communication is where I've felt the safest in this world.

This book was a labor of love by my wonderful tribe.

First and foremost, I want to thank my mother, Ella Ford, to whom this book is dedicated, for being the most loving, wonderful, and selfless person I've ever known. Thank you for saving me from myself. Thank you for keeping my secrets. Thank you for giving me a part of your greatness.

Viv and Ryan represent opposite sides of me. Viv is in essence a dissertation on my psyche. My inside self whom rarely anyone sees; whereas, Ryan is more closely aligned to my outward self while I was growing up.

Art imitates life, and art intimates life. When I finished the first draft of this book, my mom, the inspiration for both Geraldine and Henri, had not yet passed away. Viv's depression spiral was something I modeled after my own experiences; revisiting chapter twelve felt as if I were reliving her death all over again. My mother was the only person in my family who really understood my quirks and intricacies. To the rest of my family, I hope that the inner workings of Viv's mind and her logic help to explain a few things for you.

To one of the most brilliant young minds I've come across, my personal editor, Becca Levitin, thank you for challenging me to dig deeper with the characters, staying true to their essence during the editing process, and making sure the web of Viv's world was tightly wrapped.

I want to thank my sister, Kamailia Williams; my love, Alexis Parker; and my friends Amy Franklin, Ashleigh Wilson, Bianca Ashley, Demetrius Curry, Devalin Jackson, Dominique Hollins, Genesis Garcia, Jessie Rowshandel, Joii Duke, Jazzmine Duke, Kebone Moloko, Maria Aroujo, Mrnalini Mills, Naima McQueen, Nigel Sealey, Rhodes Perry, Sheneita Graham, Sonya Fox, and Travis Tanner for believing in me, encouraging me, providing feedback on the characters and story arcs, and supporting me as I navigated the same loss that Viv endured.

To my therapist, Dr. Tori Branch, thank you for sticking with me since 2013 through the ups and downs; you've helped me navigate my thoughts, understand that they are valid, and learn how they fit into the world.

To my mentor, Amanda Shareghi, thank you for reminding me that the story is fire and to always remember what a badass bitch I am.

I never thought that I'd say thank you to all my exes, past crushes, flings, and one-night stands, but without all of you this story would not exist. Regardless of how we ended, I hope you can appreciate the inclusion of your birthdays, our anniversary dates, and memories that I still look back on fondly in chapter twenty-two.

To my hometown of San Francisco and the region that raised me, thank you for being the weirdest bubble for a young, queer black girl to grow up in. This book offered a way for me to share your magic, which is only known to locals, with anyone who picks it up. There is nowhere else in the world I'd rather be from.

To the artists mentioned in the book, thank you for being brave enough to share your light with the world. Whether it's physical art or music, your creative expressions were my safe haven; they put words to things I could not say myself and helped me make sense of the world. More importantly, knowing that someone else could write those words let me know that I wasn't truly as alone as I felt.

Thank you to Jenn T. Grace for the referral to Lisa Umina. To Lisa and her team at Halo Publishing, for taking a chance on more risqué subject matter to get this book into the world.

Finally, to the reader, thank you for allowing Viv's world to be your escape from reality. I hope you go out there and Viv it up!

www.ingramcontent.com/pod-product-compliance
Lightning Source LLC
Chambersburg PA
CBHW071834020726
47502CB00004B/1354